Nikola Zaturoski

D1528207

NUMB

Edited by:

John Haas

Illustrations by:

Ric Kinon

Lulu Books

ISBN 978-1-257-95820-7

Ric and John,
Thank you.

For Emilia

First Chapter

My daydream was cut short by a tiny man on the other side of the counter. He waved his hand in front of my face until my eyes locked with his.

"Wimsley, what's up?" I asked, glaring into his painted glass eye. Wimsley tightened his eyelid around the white orb. The watery surface reflected the light hovering above us.

Wimsley grunted as we entered a staring contest. His benevolent attitude towards me had dwindled over the years. Wimsley longed for a confrontation with me after all the free drinks his coworker passed to me. "Well, drink up," he muttered. "I didn't poison it this time."

"The glass is dirty," I blinked and turned away, forfeiting the match. I never enjoyed locking eyes, it made me feel dirty. I sighed and stuck my custom-made mask back onto my head, carefully tucking in my ears.

"You're a picky little bitch, aren't you?"

I ignored his insult. "I don't feel like drinking, I guess." I took the wallet out of my jacket and paid this time. Wimsley gave me a strange look as I got up and walked out into the rain.

"Oh, right!" Wimsley wanted to give it one last shot. "All jackasses are passive-aggressive! I get it!" His laughing echoed as I slammed the door with a hidden smirk on my face.

I'm used to getting teased because of my mutated appearance. While I am mostly human, it is hard to ignore my donkey attributes. My ears, hooves, tail and mane are not polite to the eyes. The metallic miasma that appeared twenty years ago affected my birth greatly. I may not be the only mutant, but I can honestly say I would much rather live amongst the ones that heckle me than those insane activists. I exhaled and walked on.

The rain is beautiful. It is as soothing as a llama's hum, but can be very dangerous depending on the vicious metal in the air. If the droplets collect enough of the particles, it can pierce skin or even kill. If it rains heavy, it showers thousands of needles that pour forth from pin-cushion clouds and crash into the cracked tar streets, creating a gentle sound of destruction. When it snows, grenades fall from the sky. No grenades or needles today, though, it was a gentle drizzle for now.

The smell of metal lingered in my mask as I turned the street corner. It was only four more blocks; but the headache made it feel like a mile. Drinking was out of the question; some squirts of morphine and a warm shower sounded like a pleasant weekend night. By the third block I was unbuttoning my blazer, my lack of patience disturbed me.

I leaped inside the apartment and began to strip. The heavy, wet clothes clung on to me with incredible tenacity. Once I chucked the heavy mound of cotton into a nearby basket, I began the search. I explored my entire loft and found nothing. The vein on the side of my temple was pulsating with an angry vigor. I whimpered for a solid minute until I found it where it always was- inside my jacket pocket. I shrugged at the soggy bag of clear, brown pills. Without thinking I forced three tablets through my shivering lips and chewed until the inside of my mouth was coated with bland delight. I was hoping to inject it, but my quivering hands made it far too risky. My breathing slowed down. The pulse inside my head abated. When it kicked in I felt every ounce of blood tingling underneath my skin like a parade of centipedes. The magical bugs crawled within my fingertips and circulated in my brain, massaging my eyes. I shut them and turned my nose to the ceiling, the furry tip of my tail tickling my lower back. I passionately danced towards my bathroom. The sound of running water in the shower forced me to dance. I jumped into the white cubicle and raised my head to the fountain of scalding hot water. I smiled as my face melted off my skull. A few hours passed until 8 o'clock when I realized I had missed several phone calls from a few friends wondering if I was dead. By a few friends I mean less than two.

I took another one of my magic pills to amplify the effect. The television was on, but I paid no attention to it. Before I could turn it off, my phone rang again and I answered it unsteadily. On the other line was John Strub. John is tall, intelligent, and completely off his rocker. John took after his insane uncle who taught him "everything he knew". After the untimely "death" of his uncle, Bill Strub, John developed an irrational hatred towards, well, everything. However, there was something to admire about John- it definitely wasn't his lack of sanity. He lived without regrets, unlike myself, who self-pities far too often. John and I had a wondrous synergy. We clicked immediately when I moved in with him in our late teen years. His constant anti-human ranting complimented my envy for the normal man. We were always abused; John constantly picked fights that he always lost (if it is possible to call it losing- he would lay defenseless as his opponent pummeled his chuckling face in) and I was bullied to no end. John never fought back because of his firm belief in flagellation therapy, I never fought back because I was conditioned to think that I deserved such a beating. When I woke up in the middle of the night screaming in terror from the dreadful flashbacks, there was John choking on vomit moments after his dreams intoxicated him with noxious images of humanity. He is my best friend, but I would never take a bullet for him.

"Mutt, get back to the bar," John demanded over the phone. "There's a bunch of guys here that I pissed off."

I let out a long, unnecessary groan. "What did you this time?"

"They had piercings and tattoos all over them!" John breathed in heavily. I heard the mild roar of a blowtorch in the background. "I simply stated that it is too expensive to express yourself with such trivial things when knowledge is free! Don't you think they should express knowledge over pricey, extravagant material? I'm standing up for myself this time."

"That's absolutely repugna-" the phone clicked. The mask went back on.

I traveled back to Wimsley's Bar. The rain had stopped a short while ago. Chrome-colored worms surfaced from the cracks in the asphalt, then waited on the surface to die. I cautiously stepped past them on the sidewalk. Eventually I lost interest and grew careless, shifting my eyes to the clouds that remained darker than usual. The rain might return.

I did a double take when I spotted an old man on a rooftop. He was sitting on the ledge of the building, letting his feet dangle. He was either a suicide jumper or an Owl. There was no time to think about this, John could be horribly maimed by now. I couldn't miss that.

My left hoof took the first step into the dingy bar. The rest of my body followed its lead. The first thing to catch my eye upon entering was a group of deaf aging females laughing like irritated baby bats being fornicated with little twigs. They didn't stop as I stepped in. The sound made me cringe and forced me to cover my dagger-like ears as I headed to the far corner of the counter.

"John's fucking around in the bathroom," Wimsley shook his head and poured me a drink. "He scared the kiddies away. I don't know how long I can deal with him, man. He brings in a crowd, but he scares so many away."

This was my chance to get on his good side for free drinks without absorbing insults. "Hey, man, no sweat. Why would you want a bunch of trouble-hungry punks anyway?"

Wimsley nodded agreeably. "True, true. You ever see how John draws the crowd in with his flaming sword swallowing act?" I nodded back at him as he continued. "I can't stay mad at him."

Wimsley was nothing more than an aging hippie. He had plenty of money from his contracting years. Wealth was never a problem, no matter how often he complained about money. He was pretty old, but well-built and had several blood transfusions to keep himself healthy. Wimsley was too old to revel in our era, but too young to settle down and die.

The deaf females continued telling jokes through hand gestures. I shook my head and took a seat right under the television, attempting to drown out the mindless laughing and finger snaps with boxing commentators. I removed the gas mask from my face and downed the shot of whiskey and asked for another. A warm, gentle finger petted the brim of my ear. The finger felt as moist as the atmosphere outside. It was slender and relaxing.

"Mutt?" a delicate voice said. "You're still alive."

You're still alive. The words scraped the back of my spine. Her name is Mary, my first and only ex-girlfriend. After she dumped me, I often thought why someone so beautiful would date someone like me, especially where bedroom matters were concerned. Perhaps she pitied me; I mean, my appearance could be described as grotesque. My best guess was that she was a complete pervert.

Such a pervert, in fact, she created a clone of herself. She dumped me to go fuck herself.

Cloning was introduced forty years ago. The two types, extrachomosomal and recombinant, have torn a hole into morality and vastly changed the behavior of mankind. It is the sinner's invention that ushered in an era of sex minions and slavery.

Extrachromosomal was used to raise a human from birth, which takes longer to hatch and is much more expensive. The "extras" were technically more real than the recombinants, but people seldom ever made these. It was just an alternative for parents that could not bare children and refused to adopt.

Recombinants should be considered a new culture or race. Their blood is a clear and thick surrogate that must be rejuvenated every three years. Their "oil change" is very expensive, but they are immune to every illness, are medically simple to operate on, and can modify their physical structure to look wildly different and perform incredible super human tasks. This was Mary's choice.

I never met her clone; she never dared mutter her name to me, either. I can only guess that it looked exactly like her. The thought of two perfect creatures in front of my eyes made my heart pound. Ever since she left me, I had a secret hatred towards clones. Love was no longer a blind thing. It is now analyzed in a lab, shit out by a machine, and handed out like a prescription. Mary continued to stare me down. I couldn't help but wonder why. I'm sure her clone would happily pleasure her all day.

She began rocking my rickety stool with her little black boot, waiting for my answer in anticipation. Ignoring her was not an option, and the first glance of her bare legs that emerged from her little black dress made my chest ache. I shifted my seat and looked into her watery eyes; diabolical and charming, my vision was thrown at her shockingly white canines. Every detail of her face reflected her predatory personality.

"How's the twin?" I said out of spite. She released a tiny giggle from her belly; the smell of alcohol was lingering on her laugh as she closed in for a whisper.

"Getting a check-up," she said, "She'll be away in Newark for a few days. 'Till then, I'm very much alone." I felt her coming closer, her breast pressing against my shoulder now.

My will to ignore her was fading. I knew I still cared for her. It just pissed me off to hell that she always got what she wanted. I stared at the television set perched in the far corner of the room. A live coverage was on the news, something about a man having sex with some other dead guy across the state. The reporter was crouching next to a shallow grave, pointing at the bare-assed victim inverted in a humiliating position. The casket was smashed and pieces of it stuck out of the poor cadaver. The image didn't bother me much. The dead are as common as the living. I looked to my right and saw Mary was watching too. She lost interest and put her full concentration back onto me.

"Sick world, eh?" She said. "You would be surprised what some people would do for pleasure."

"I bet it was the same guy from last week," Wimsley interrupted. "His AIDS stricken boyfriend died and he snuck into the morgue for a final stiff fuck. I guess he didn't wanna let go."

The gas mask was shaking in my fingertips as I finally gave in to her innocent smile. "Okay, Mary, you found me. What could you possibly want? Wimsley, give me a fucking beer."

"You got it," he said with a wink. His false eye twinkled with a newly found respect for me. Wimsley was there when I first met Mary. He was enthralled by her charm, just like every other guy. I was too, but chose to ignore her. That's what lured her to me- the ounce of false resistance sparked an interest, exactly like this moment.

"Mutt..." Her leg was entwined with one of mine. I felt the blood rushing into my heart. The morphine pumped through my veins and withered away.

"And what's with these fucking stools? Can we paste a back on them and call it a fucking chair!" I haven't been this nervous since she left me. Mary giggled at my outburst. I violently shook my head. My eyes managed to scan the room well enough to tell me that, aside from the deaf bats, that we were all alone.

"Come on, let's play," she said as she pulled on her elastic garter. "We can go back to your-"

A crashing sound startled both of us as John retracted his boot from the swinging bathroom door with a revolting look on his face. The crashing of a thousand drums echoed in my head when I noticed the fire blazing from his eyes.

"John, that blowtorch isn't on you, is it?" Wimsley cried.

John snapped out of his power trip and tried to play it cool. "Oh, hey buddy. My barbiturates are wearing off, got anything on you?" He caught Mary staring him down. "Am I interrupting anything?" The rain picked up again.

I untied my leg from Mary's, "not at all."

Did the necrophiliac wear protection? Find out after this...

The llama's hum turned into a cicada's shriek. Outside, the sound of scattering footsteps could be heard...

Second Chapter

John stayed silent as he closed up the bar. He had to flick the lights on and off so the deaf could get the idea. They got up and walked out, giggling to each other as they communicated with hand gestures. Wimsley walked out from the storage room that he was inside of for a few minutes. "Go on home, Wim, I'll take care of it." Wimsley nodded and walked out into the violent rain with an umbrella made out of a strong metal. It sounded like a crash symbol pelted furiously with dried rice.

"I'll be back," Mary said. "I have to use a bathroom." She got up and walked down the murky hallway. Her stride was elegant and repulsive. It didn't matter how tawdry she was, I was still attracted to her. John and I heard the bathroom door open and close.

John turned to me after he closed the window blinds. "Impudent strumpet," he said under his breath. "Impudent strumpet!" John spit out a glob of yellow saliva on the floor. He gently grabbed my wrist and tapped at it with his other hand. "She got you into that stuff. She only uses you for kicks!"

"Maybe she's changed," I said unsteadily.

"Yeah, and maybe this time she won't fellate you with a scorpion in her mouth!"

A sloppy shiver coursed through me. John stared at me with relief when he noticed the words had a serious effect on me. "She's just a pervert! You're part donkey; I bet she's into bestiality. Yeah, that must be it."

"Don't even act like you never-"

He interrupted me. "Okay, okay. I take that one back."

"She'll be joining us tonight," I muttered. John nodded, accepting defeat. It surprised me how fast he backed down this time. I lit a cigarette and handed it to him with a thank you.

"You owe me," he said with a puff.

Mary must have been listening through the walls. The second John exhaled his smoke Mary opened the door and returned to her seat while seductively biting her lip. John rolled his eyes as he counted the change in the register. I stared in awe at his incredible speed. If his bill-counting didn't impress me enough, he grabbed a handful of quarters, tossed them into the air, and listened as the coins crashed on the counter. "6.25!" he shouted.

Mary clapped for him. "You are a sorcerer of true reckonings!" John cracked a little smile, then, shook it off.

The front door blasted open. A large man entered the bar with his face hidden in his reinforced rain coat. Water dripped off his hood and shoulders and landed in tiny pools at the entrance. The sound of his deep breathing made us all feel uneasy.

John turned to the man without hesitation, "Sorry buddy, we're closing early for no reason at all."

He locked the door behind him and pulled the damp hood off his head. His massive orange beard wiggled as he turned towards us. The ends of his hair were a discolored dark brown. It was Gleesty. He lifted his large hand for a wave. Gleesty's sausage-like fingers cast a shadow over our bodies.

Gleesty had an interesting way about him. He loved fantasy and videogames; anything that dealt with combat or mythology, really. Nordic lore and history was his specialty. Gleesty studied battles, drank heavily, and oddly enough, was one of the kindest fellows I've ever come across. His intentions were always benevolent, the mirror opposite of John or I.

"Oh, sorry, I was looking for the douchebag convention," Gleesty yelled, relaxing his enormous shoulders.

"Ah, the deranged pachyderm has arrived," John said, smiling.

Gleesty flung his coat on a table and sat next to Mary and me. The smell of wet leather lingered around him. He patted my shoulder with his gigantic hand, almost toppling me to the ground while letting out a deep, jovial laugh. Once I got used to the smell of leather, the smell of alcohol was introduced, protruding through his neck and making my eyes water.

"What's your story?" John poured him a glass of whiskey.

"Eh, same old," Gleesty said. "Looking for junk around the area to sell as scrap metal. 'Still playing that online game, been thinking about joinin' the military." Gleesty looked at Mary and I and smiled. "Little buddy, nice lady friend you got there."

Mary grinned, charmed by the grizzly bear in front of her. "My name's Mary, I'm an old friend of Mutt's."

John dragged the sole of his foot on the ground, making a horrible squeaking noise. I hissed at him.

"You can call me Glee," he said. "I am a new friend of Mutt's, met back in the hos-"

I knew I was trying too hard to keep a good impression on Mary when I interrupted Gleesty with a cough. It developed into an awkward silence, which John embraced with closed eyes. To make matters worse, the rain stopped. I saw Mary's grin growing wider in my peripherals. Thankfully, Gleesty broke the ice.

"Where we goin' tonight?" he asked.

I was worried that John had changed his mind for my torment. Mary and I stared at him for the answer. He frowned when he said "Mutt's". The burden was lifted off my back. I handed John another cigarette as a reward.

Gleesty looked at me and smiled. "Are ya bringin' your lady friend with ya?"

I nodded and felt Mary's hand creeping up onto my own. I saw John's knuckles turn white at the corner of my eye. Guilt crept into the back of my skull. However, Gleesty liked her, I liked her, and Mary stays from the popular vote.

"Let's get a move on then," said Gleesty. "Before the rail spikes get us."

John fired out a conversation to try and stall us. He *wanted* lethal rain to pierce Mary. "Glee, you hear about the necro down at the cemetery?"

"Eh?" Gleesty grunted. "Oh, oh no, I have not. Big deal. It's not unusual these days."

John pouted. He tried his very best to stop us from reaching our destination. "Yeah, but he fucked his AIDS infested boyfriend! I bet after the dead cells and irradiated blood, the STD turns into ultra-AIDS! Super AIDS! The vulgar atrocities! Our lives are at stake! We must stay here!"

Gleesty laughed, grabbed his large coat and threw it over his shoulder. "Well, we all can't be as charming as you, John. Let's go."

The four of us walked out without saying another word. We examined the horizon, then the streets. The blend of gritty industry and nature's common cycle made the outside look like a melting Hell. It was no surprise to us all except for Gleesty; his giant eyeballs glaring at the environment and putting his steps to a halt. "Shit man."

John gave up on making us stay. He patted Glee's enormous back. "Come on, it's getting dark."

We quietly walked down the first few streets, gas masks hugging our faces. Everyone was anxious to get to my apartment. Mary concentrated on the cracks in the sidewalk. John and Gleesty kicked a rock around to occupy themselves.

Gleesty took his mask off. "Just rained, it's not that bad now." The three of us removed ours as well. The air wasn't bad, so I lit a cigarette.

"Is it hard walking all the way over here from another town?" John asked Gleesty.

"I actually enjoy it," Gleesty said. "Some punks actually tried to jump me while coming here today. I grabbed one of 'em and slammed his back on the pavement. Tore off his mask and crammed his skull between a catch basin, watched him chew on the iron panel."

"And the other punks?" John started to smile. His thirst for violence shimmered in his eyes. John played games with Gleesty fairly often. Most of the time they were strategy games, seldom were they ever trivia. Gleesty played conservatively, while John was liberal and aggressive, often shouting when he got too into the game.

"Ran off, I followed them for a little while though. Their friend is probably still trapped in that iron."

"Adorable."

I looked up and saw several people sitting on rooftops watching us. I knew exactly who they were. The same man dangling his feet earlier was with his friends.

I smiled up at them and shouted, "gooble, gobble, the end is nigh!" They blankly looked down at me. Normally, they would smile back and say something outrageously strange. Something was not right, but nothing is ever right with these lunatics. We continued walking, attempting to suppress the silence.

We call these people Owls. Owls sit on their rooftops almost all day and night observing their surroundings. They sit right above the rust fog, safe from danger. These antisocial outcasts take pleasure in watching everything die slowly from the poison underneath them. While their lifestyle is simple, their philosophy is complex and absurd. Their large, leathery eyes and droopy faces reflect on their dull attires and dry personalities.

The Owls have set up an odd anti-culture subculture when the war occurred over two decades ago. Their dangerous motives are cerebral and subtle. They are not some kind of psychopathic Jehovah's Witnesses; they are atheists with one sole purpose: to bury everything with them and to keep it there. They demand technology should come to a halt, and the human race, or, the "morbidly-obese plague," should be exterminated. Owls are anti-history fundamentalists, corrupting minds of children with false knowledge in order to shatter their brains. They attacked the museums that they own; destroying their own property inside and creating new pieces constantly. They want music obliterated as well. Anything that can express one's soul they have tainted. Many think it's just for kicks, some think it's just a gimmick for attention. But someone out there knew exactly what they had in mind. John's uncle knew the true reason of their actions. He was an Owl too, and the strangest of them all.

John told me the story of how Bill Strub was "accepted" into this tiny cult that littered the east coast. He walked into one of their music festivals- which did not involve any instruments, just humming. They called it the Ad Libitum Festival. Thousands of them were humming on the shores of a beach. Mr. Strub claimed he walked in front of them, and the second a single one noticed who he was, they bowed their heads and welcomed him with open arms. Old Owl Strub had many secrets that he carried with him. We were lucky enough to pry one out of him. When we confronted him about the truth of the Owls, he answered us with a dignity he's never shown to anyone. "These anti-mongers have figured out how to unlock the secrets of life-why we are here and what purpose we serve. They are on the right page by being in the wrong book. Instead of using logic to understand life, they are going to opposite direction. The less sense they make, the more they learn. Being against art, history, music and life will subtract all the noise and the wrong directions to the point where they find the truth. They are tired of breakthroughs and the linear reality. These folks don't even like the use of language! They are the negative oracles, and they predict the future by canceling out the present and altering the past.

Everyone wants truth. Why not untruth? Uncertainty? Ignorance? Ask Nietzsche, ask the Sphinx, ask the bloody mirror. For rebirth. The stupid are fresh and immortal, the smart shall wither."

When Bill joined the Owls, they all worshiped him like a mentor. Mind you, most of the original Owls worked under Gleesty's parents years ago. Most of them were fired and blacklisted for "crimes against the human spirit." Bill was also exiled this way. These scientists were paid very highly, and after they were fired, many changed their identities and became these Dada hermits. I am unsure if they changed names for security purposes, or if it just blends with their other odd beliefs.

Third Chapter

I first met Bill Strub when he and John moved across the street from my old house. I remember crossing the street over for the first time and knocking on their door for a decent hello, back when my parents were not dead and rotting. The door opened and a middle-aged man stared at me dead in the eyes. He grabbed me by the shoulders and threw me inside the house. The smell of dried carrots strongly permeated the dwelling. The walls were torn down and replaced with thousands of stiff, worn books. Clocks and buckets were hanging from the top of the ceiling. Bill grabbed my shoulders and spun me around.

"Once you dare a peek of this place, you will never stop staring," he said, constantly looking over at the ticking clocks. "I often have to change their batteries. Not many people remember what batteries are anymore."

"I, I know what batteries are," I said. He made it seem like they were outdated and forgotten; a man truly ahead of his time.

Bill smiled and took off my mask. "Perfect. John, come see our neighbor! Oh, allow me to introduce my entity. I am William O. Strub, a Quantum Alchemist."

John emerged from the labyrinth of books. His body slithered near the tower of tomes as if he was attached to them. He looked frightened and nervous; his delicate eyes looked directly at my face and, unlike many kids, he did not look away in disgust.

"Well met," he said. His voice was tender and mild. "I'm John."

"Hi," I replied. John looked directly into my eyes; it was from that moment on we connected like brothers.

"How cute," Bill said. He waved his hand in the air in a shamanistic manner. "I wrote almost all of these books, even the phone books." I looked over to the massive pile, most of them being school books that I once read- only their covers were scratched out in marker and written over with *ANOTHER VOLUME OF BILL STRUBBERY.* "Well, my dears, I'm going up top. You boys are welcome to come up once you are both acquainted."

My brain told me run out the door and never look back, but my heart wanted to stay. They were the nicest, warmest people I have met. They treated me like a human, and even took care of me when I was sick. I felt that I made the right choice by staying.

Bill climbed an old wooden ladder through two holes from the top floors. John looked at me and sighed in relief.

"Good," he said. "He likes you."

I stared at John in befuddlement, "What *is* he?"

"He's my uncle, one of the smartest men in the world. He is trying to kill us all. I'm his apprentice and he is teaching me secrets."

"What kind of secrets?"

"I really am not sure. Come up top with me, maybe he feels that I am ready to know. You are my first friend, after all."

We climbed up the ladder and through the hole in the roof. At first glance we witnessed Bill, completely naked, masturbating furiously at the edge of the roof. His toes clenched the tips of the building. A plugging device was lodged in his anal orifice. He moaned, his left arm extending into the air like an antenna as he shivered with an exploding orgasm. His semen dripped off the rooftop and disappeared into the light fog. He turned around and smiled to us. In a nutshell, Bill got off to the thought of chaos, biblical catastrophes, and imagining the fall of mankind. He was a misanthropist and an apocalyptic sadist.

"Incredible!" he said. "This land is perfect! We're just above this terrible fog. Tell me, boy, what is your name?"

"Mutt," I said as I stared at his naked body. While his face and hands appeared withered and fragile, the rest of his body was extremely muscular. He was in better shape than anyone I have ever met. It was eerie, seeing him naked and intimidating, but I also felt safe.

"Now, Mutt. You can either love life or love hating life. Anything in between is too queer for mankind. Fall in between and you will often ask yourself questions that you will never find an answer to. Understand?"

I was far too confused and scared to speak, so I just nodded.

Bill put his clothes back on and sat down on a chair, looking at me, hardly blinking. "Tell me, young lad, have you heard of my studies?"

I made a squeak and tilted my head.

"Makes sense, I was kicked out of CERN and the university I taught at because of my dark and dangerous knowledge- and don't get me started on those Goresmiths." He shook his head with a smile on his face, his reminiscing put him in an ecstatic rage. "I was one of the first humans to create an anti-hydrogen particle. I began my studies with elementary quanta at around your age, and with the help of a lightning storm that fried the frontal lobes of my brain, I grew more and more interested in the field." Bill stood up and reached down the backside of his pants, pulling out the fornication device. "Whoops, forgot about that. I'm still stuck in the anal stage. Oh, that Sigmund Freud." Bill stuck the fornication device into his mouth, and it was then I realized it was a pipe. "Oh, and oral stage. And the phallic stage, as you witnessed earlier." He constantly changed the topic, it was nearly impossible to follow his thinking process. It was all coming too fast from different angles.

"Sir," John said. "You digress."

Bill smiled. "Oh, right, right. Creating anti-particles takes very long, is very expensive, and is very hard to contain. In fact, creating a few thousand of those particles, which can't even fill a tiny balloon would take years, and I do not have that kind of fucking time, kid."

I opened my mouth to speak. "What are you trying to acc-"

"Patience, patience. I grew more and more interested in quantum physics, or anything absurd, really. But physics was my main field of study. Thermodynamics was a great part in my work, I was in love with the second law. Entropy. Know it, kid? After creating several anti-hydrogen quarks, I built a tiny room and worked on tiny tiny animals. Kinetic energy and death lead to my affair with entropy. And sex. I worked on the simplest of creatures: the termite. If I performed my procedure correctly, I could accelerate their evolution process in this outdated universe and convert them into beings of pure, powerful energy. I created many of them! I called them entromites! Think about it- tiny, pure, glowing little beings of light! Immortal! Eating at our universe, first taking out wood, the most innocent of all beings."

My mouth swung open. I couldn't believe what this psychopath was saying. He smiled at my reaction.

"Yes! But these little *fucks* escaped the room that I spawned them in and began fucking around in my walls! I heard *CRCHT CRCHT* sounds all night," he said, while twisting his fists in opposite motions. He stomped his feet angrily. "I had to take the damn walls down to try and capture them, but no luck. I guess they died, they weren't perfect. That's why we moved here, I took apart our last home, is that not correct, Johnny?"

John nodded.

Bill stood up and rubbed John's shoulders as an act of respect. "I found him crying underneath a pylon, my brother was killed flying a kite with him. As for his mother, who knows. Moving on, I grew fascinated when cloning came about. I took two specimens, John here, and a female. John lent me his sperm so I could convert it to a negative life form so I can artificially inseminate her to create an anti-human. And once John here shook hands with his child, boom. Unfortunately, the girl died during the process, heh. The negative sperm caused an implosion, and it was very difficult to create an anti-ovary to hold it in place inside a typical incubator. It would've been...anticlimactic!" Bill burst out with laughter and then cleared his throat.

"Anyway, all of this would be too much work, and there must be an easier way to create my master plan."

"Which is?" I asked.

"To create the most sophisticated anti-particle, one so rare and powerful, that just one would cancel out the universe! To make nothing out of an everything! The anti-god quark!"

I felt nauseous. John looked at me in fear. "But, why do that?"

Bill Strub laughed. "Because, this universe is tainted, my child. Nothing is pure; even milk turns sour before it chalks. If I create a completely indifferent solution to this place, a new, more perfect world would sprout out of the former one's ashes. It's not that I hate this universe, I just love it so much that I must put it out of its misery."

From my first few minutes with him, to the last few years, Bill told me many strange ideas that I didn't bother to comprehend. John was his student. However, I think even John had trouble understanding his philosophy.

The rest of the day ended with John and me cowering in a corner, drugged up on ayahuasca while Bill entertained us with shadow puppets.

John would later grow up and constantly mumble quotes by his mad uncle.

Bill Strub supposedly died during my time in a rehabilitation center. His heart went towards the same direction his brain did. In his death bed, he gave John a lock box. Bill explained that inside the box are the answers to the truth about life, the secrets of happiness and everything that he ever wanted to know. John just has to find the key somewhere in this world, which could be anything. His last words were, "Follow the Owls."

The problem is that the only person to see Bill Strub dead was John. Also, the room that they were in was filled with a strange hallucinogenic smoke. Bill enjoyed meditating with John. Bill also enjoyed drugging John during their time alone together. Bill Strub's body disappeared when John woke up the next day. He believes that his body had undergone so much stress from his strenuous life that it went on into a black hole, attempting to convert itself into an anti-dark matter particle. It was "explained" in a letter his uncle wrote during the meditation session. Or something.

Fourth Chapter

Everyone seemed to relax a little more once we reached my street. Mary slid her fingers between mine. We didn't bother speaking; breathing outside without the taste of sulfur on the tip of our tongues was a rare event. We all took breaths as if we had been trapped for several minutes underwater. Gleesty was the first to speak.

"Feels good," he said, as his heavy breathing continued. "Used to be, it was healthy to breathe outside."

"Who needs health?" John said.

Gleesty chuckled. "I suppose I'm not healthy in any shape, mentally or physically."

"Happiness is more important than sanity." John twitched and muttered something incomprehensible.

Gleesty thought about this for a second, then shrugged once we reached my stairs. I unlocked my door and let the stooges in first. Mary caressed my body lightly, much like the fog, before stepping inside.

John looked at my key and thought for a second. Then shook his head.

All of us headed straight to the living room and chucked our masks at the nearest wall. John sat down on the couch. Gleesty turned the television on and sat down next to him. The silence lingered as we focused our attention on the television. A classic cartoon of a coyote attempting to outwit and catch a road runner was on.

"I always wondered," Gleesty chuckled. "Will Wile E. Coyote ever catch that bloody thing?"

"I used to watch this cartoon all the time," John said.

"With your wacky uncle?" I said with a smile.

"With him, yes." John exhaled and relaxed his fingers on the couch.

"From the perspective of the family, we feel that art is one of the greatest languages that humans have to offer. And it is not straight forward, no. It is abstract. It is hidden in the artwork's guts.

"Wile E. Coyote is the perfect example; a legendary character shit out through the intestines of Chuck Jones. A symbolic meaning is here, and it relates to mankind as a whole. Throughout the coyote's reign, which, during the same days this cartoon was made, real life events of competition were taking place, such as the Olympics. Anyway, he sought after one goal: capturing and eating the road runner. Every single person relates to this. We are alone in a remote universe within ourselves, searching to accomplish a dream. The problem is, our road runners are goals that are often underestimated. They exceed our expectations. Now, a simple animal that could be caught easily would not fulfill our standards. We don't want anything too easy or there will not be any satisfaction. Only disappointment. And we are always hungry. When we eat our meal, we will only be hungry for another dream. And if we plunge to our doom from a cliff, or fall into the path of a moving train, or blow ourselves up, we tend to bounce back. Our goals can be a force to be reckoned with, but humans are also resilient.

"And now look at him. He made a giant robotic version of himself. Can it be man creating God? It is an image of himself, and he is deluding himself into false hope, is he not?"

I glanced at the television. I saw the road runner dodging a cliff and luring the coyote off the ledge. A whistle sounded, followed by a splat with a puff of gray smoke. John giggled at the screen and Mary and Gleesty frowned, saddened by the cruel fate of the animated entity.

I asked John, "What's the E stand for?"

"Ethelbert!"

"Any subtle meaning to that?" Mary asked.

"It's the name of some fucking king." John looked away from the television and began making shadow puppets.

"Hmph," I stared at the cartoon for a few seconds, examining the coyote's long wrinkled snout and his beady little eyes. It suddenly hit me. "I knew a guy that looked exactly like him."

"Mutant?" John asked.

"Yeah."

"Where? The Zoo?" Everyone chuckled.

"M.A."

Gleesty wrinkled his forehead, his eyebrows darted down towards me. "What?" His face went back to normal. "Oh."

"Yeah, Mutants Anonymous." I looked over at Mary who was holding back her laughter. Her bright red cheeks were ready to explode. John glared at her, filling the room with his vibe. I suppose he thought he was the only one allowed to tease me.

She squeaked and covered her face with a pillow, "Was he fucking a bird?"

My memories suddenly grew more vivid. "Actually... yes, there was a female there that had a beak."

John laughed, brushing the anger away. "So he stuffed her like a turkey, eh?"

Gleesty giggled violently. "What exactly did you do at those meetings?"

I stood up to light a cigarette, inhaled, and laid back down in my seat. "We spoke about how pitiful we were, how upset we were with our appearances. We held hands and chanted words to raise our esteem and all of that other fancy shit. But that was only the beginning.

"We recited George Orwell's Animal Farm and how it was our sign to strike back at the human race for oppressing us. We crowed, squealed, hissed, and barked at the smooth-faced, average humans. The Pig was the one that really had an impact on me. He would often pull out fashion magazines and paste the heads of barnyard creatures onto them. I remember that gruesome snout of his- full of piercings and hardened over with dried snot. He was the activist of the lot."

Mary had a look of terror in her eyes. She grabbed my cigarette and took a drag, ashed it, and stuck it back between my fingers.

"We also talked about breaking into sperm banks and replacing all the semen with ours. The group name we used was the Mad Cow Cult; the ten of us felt it had a nice ring to it. It was me, The Pig, The Dog, The Cat, The Horse, The Goose, The Goat, The Cow and The Rat. We never used our real names.

"And what happened?"

"A lot of things happened. Some of us didn't agree with the strange plans, others prepared for it, up to the point where The Pig wrote a code of ethics and created tons of plans. To me, he was all talk. The Cat was the most interesting one in my eyes. He rarely spoke, he was so kind, yet he went through so much in his life. He told us that he had died multiple times already, and claimed to have nine lives.

"Then, the person who held the meetings, an over-sized bullfrog, croaked. We didn't have anyone else to make us coffee. My parents died at around the same time." John nodded his head with a large smile.

"Hm?" Gleesty raised an eyebrow. "What's John know about this?"

I smiled. "His uncle adopted me for the last two years before I turned eighteen."

Gleesty shook his head with disgust at John. John smiled back.

"But there are plenty of Mutant groups around, why didn't you join any of them? You coulda gotten paychecks from the government."

"Yeah, I was going to join one that wanted to settle all the mutants out on an island, it didn't catch my eye. It seemed a lot like 'The Island of Dr. Moreau'."

"Some of them were scams anyway," John said. "One of those organizations sent all mutants to a slaughterhouse."

"Who's Bill Strub?" Mary asked.

"No idea," said Gleesty. "They've shown me some of his writings right around the day he passed away. Funny guy."

"That's terrible. When did he die?"

"Six months ago, was it?" Gleesty looked at John, who kept nodding.

Fifth Chapter

I was in the other room with her faster than my mind could realize it. The last thing I recall clearly was her snagging a handful of pills from the table and grabbing my hand. I was escorted to the bedroom, the scent of her bitter perfume following between us. She stopped me in front of my bedroom door, removed her clothing, and hung them on the doorknob. It was her little "do not disturb" sign.

When I fell onto the bed, everything became an awful blur accompanied by an obnoxious ringing in my ears. Hues of purple and yellow trailed behind Mary while she danced gracefully in front of me. She turned to the wall, guiding her shadow to mine. Its long fingers pierced my chest and caused me to writhe violently as she assaulted my shadow.

My two friends went about their own conversation. I could hear their muffled voices from the room over.

Mary's sultry dance put in me a trance. She rotated slowly, examining my plain white room. All I had was a bed, a window, and a dresser with a chess board set up on it. Before she completed her full rotation, we both glared at a silverfish eating a moth on a wall. I looked back to our shadows, still romantically entangled. Hers was a colossus compared to mine; it was sinister and angry, revealing her true form.

The drug inside of me was fading. Sweat was pouring down my face from the comedown. I had no clue how I was going to hold an erection. Mary caught my moment of withdrawal and slipped a pill between my lips. I swallowed and immediately identified the pill: Amyl Nitrate. Everything grew vivid and bright. I darted my eyes left and right, examining the room from behind Mary, triggered by inner turmoil and paranoia. Mary smiled.

"Can I get a jump start?" She said, smiling.

"I don't have the proper equipment," I said.

"...It's in the purse."

"The boys will hear us. They didn't seem too happy with me inviting you over in the first place."

"We'll just have to keep quiet." Mary reached inside her bag and pulled out a little object. The first half of the toy was a rubber pipe with a thin little stick hiding in the center. The other half had the width of a half dollar, and about six inches in length altogether. A clear plastic strap was attached somewhere in the middle. I quietly wrapped it around my waist before shivering with delight.

"Are you ready?" she asked.

Our sex is unique. The instrument, nicknamed the lawn dart, is ridiculously dangerous. It's the only sex toy banned in seventeen states. The thin piece is designed to fit inside the urethra, the base part inside the uterus. Once activated by giving it a twist, it will vibrate and electrocute Mary and me as we fuck. The longer we go, the more dangerous it becomes. Induced with drugs, electricity, pleasure and pain, not one cell is inactive during our intercourse. Once we reach orgasm, our hearts overload and stop for a few seconds, giving us the most remarkable feeling every time. Our brains release euphoric chemicals, and adrenaline is released once we pass out. We normally wake up from our short deaths wallowing in our own shit and other various bodily fluids. I often think that this is the only reason why Mary chose me as a lover. I was open to this kind of stuff.

I stripped my clothes alongside Mary and playfully kicked around until I heard a tear. My hooves ripped the bed sheet again. I ignored it, rolled onto Mary, and crammed the lawn dart inside of me. She twisted the top and stuck it inside herself, grunting with pleasure. The vibration activated in five seconds, slow at first, following the rhythm of my thrusting. I watched myself slip inside of her. She began breathing heavily as the electricity coursed through our sex organs. I stared into her eyes, eyelashes thick and long as cricket thighs. I pressed my lips against hers for a few seconds then broke free as the burning sensation began to build. Sweat poured out of our faces as the sex toy reached its maximum level. Grinding and buzzing noises pierced our ears, accompanied by the creaking of the bed. I went faster and faster; each breath was a death rattle. Entropy flowed through our veins, sweat raining down onto the device, emitting sparks and singeing the tiny hairs on our torsos. Air was taken over by the smell of burnt flesh.

Her neck muscles twitched and she let out joyous gasps. I grabbed her white stockings and tore away at them in an electric sex frenzy.

Someone in the other room turned up the volume on the television. A live news broadcast was on...

"Fucking checkmate!" She screamed while digging her fingernails into my shoulders. She yelled it every single time we did it-it was my favorite part of the experience; her howling those words always put a smile on my face. I felt the blood trickling down my back as I burst into an orgasm and collapsed next to her. The little blonde shiny hairs stood up from her neck, bursting through the little pools of sweat that collected on her skin. My life force emptied into her body through an electrical surge. Death is truly nothing more than an orgasm.

Spurts of semen highlighted in the amber moonlight. Sperm zapped down onto her protruding hip bones. Our pupils dilated, falling into the expanding abyss.

Sixth Chapter

I see the Earth, covered in the miasma. The crust of the planet is muddied by the sludge underneath our feet. The oceans are filled with mercury. I plummet faster toward the surface.

Looking up, I can see the bitter sky oozing out large gobs of black gunk. The sticky dark mucus falls quicker than me, trailing straight down to the planet. The tar giggles as it rains down. The stars look away, ashamed for the large hunk of rock and its occupants. Galaxies laugh. The universe is filled with befuddlement.

I break through the clouds and inhale my first breath of air. It tastes like gasoline. I exhale and hold my breath, refusing to breathe in again.

The Earth grows dark. It is nothing more than a black rock. The darkness consumes the rest of matter; it is nearly impossible for me to see anything. I am falling slower. A black web catches me and cradles. As I struggle, tears pour out of my eyes from frustration. The tears burn away the web and I drift closer to the Earth.

Minutes pass. I should have reached the ground by now. I glance up, hoping the stars will return. When I look back down, I see a tiny white light miles away. I approach it slowly. My vision doesn't look away from it. I hardly blink. A tail emerges from the white ball of light.

It shoots out and passes under my legs and solidifies. I fall onto it; it feels exactly like a soft, silk curtain. It guides me to my destination. It's only a few feet away. The light is almost blinding now, but I keep my eyes on it.

I halt once again when I reach this solid circle of light. I extend my hand out to touch it, and a hand emerges from the bright shell. The curtain shoots down to the black planet. My companion accompanies me further down.

The long sheet of light transforms into a shining waterfall. The light source doesn't let go of my hand. The light reflects upon the surface of the shadow. We plunge into the dark water, purifying it instantly. The light conquers the blackness, traveling around the entire world, eliminating every bit of black it touches. The sludge deteriorates and crumbles. I am once again blinded by the powerful light.

The Earth rumbles in joy. The stars look over to see what's going on. The galaxies huddle together to witness what has happened. The universe gently smiles.

I open my eyes and take a breath. The air is so pure that it makes me lightheaded. The mist has evaporated. The trees dance in fury and joy. The oceans swish in their clear form. The rain is no longer painful. Everything is back to what the photographs contained from the old days. Pure beauty.

I turn around and see the most horrific thing in my entire life: A man attached to a giant tree. His ears are withered and fragile like dead leaves. His skin is waxy. The stomach is torn open, entrails and insects pouring out and crawling back inside the holes in his feet and wrists. He looks at me and sighs. A smile is drawn on his lips.

I attempt to swim away, but am slowly sinking. He pulls himself off the cross and approaches me on top of the water. My voice is missing when I try to scream. He lifts me from the ocean and points to my ears, then to my eyes, and then to my heart.

He carries me onto land and sets me down. The insects fly out of his body and swarm the land and sea. Fish jump out of the water and chomp at the bugs hovering above the ocean. Frogs emerge from the tiny ponds and grow wings.

The man smiles at the oldest form of beauty in the world. We walk into the forest.

Mammals scurry about and greet us with their acorns.

And then, the Earth rumbles once more. Clay hands punch through the dirt and men formed from the crust walk among us. My friend who created all of this shook his head slightly.

These newly formed men leap on top of my friend and tear at his flesh with their stone teeth. The man moans and slowly disappears into nothing. The mud creatures become flesh.

"So bright."

Seventh Chapter

When I opened my eyes I witnessed heavy waves of crimson and shit-brown; Mary was gone, no surprise there. My vision smoothed out as soon as the aroma of dried bile hit my nose. I rolled off my bed, slammed my head on the nightstand, and vomited on my floor. Then I heard a commotion coming from the living room.

I heard John first. "Anymore keys?!"

Gleesty roared. "No! Forget that thing and give us a hand!"

The sound of furniture being slammed against the wall caused me to get up from the floor and dart into the other room. Nearly everything in my apartment was put up as a barricade in front of the windows and the door. Dried blood was smeared on the walls. Fingers and a few limbs were scattered in the living room. Other objects were lying all over the ground. I grabbed a tablet of morphine from the table and shoved it in my mouth. I tripped on a cheese grater coated in flesh as I approached Mary and Gleesty peering out the window. John laid on the couch ramming a screw driver in his little lock box.

"What the hell are you guys doing?" I said.

Gleesty and Mary jumped in surprise and turned to my direction.

"Holy shit man," Gleesty said. "We thought you were dead."

"This is what you all planned on doing when I die?"

Mary shrugged and turned back to the window.

They were testing my patience. "What the fuck is going on?"

"It finally happened," John said.

I wrinkled my nose. My fists tightened into a ball. "What the *fuck* are you all doing?! Whose body parts are these? Why is my furniture *not* receiving the proper attention it deserves and why is John so fucking *strange*?!"

"Mutt," Mary said. "Come take a look, and stay quiet."

I stomped my hooves over to the window and lifted up the curtain. Peering out the window I saw nothing but pandemonium. Buildings were on fire. Cars were also caught in the conflagrations. Screams of help could be heard, followed by gunshots. I looked in the middle of the street and witnessed entrails and limbs sitting in large pools of blood. Some people were scattered in the street, walking without any energy or direction. Some of the torpid humans committed cannibalism in front of my very eyes. I gazed toward the sky and watched smoke collect above the rust fog. The sirens emerged along with the helicopters racing across the sky.

Mary grabbed my hand. "Now do you understand?"

"Looks like a normal day on Earth to me."

John laughed as Mary pulled me away from the window. "Don't let them see us."

"So what? It's a riot. Big deal. Grab your shovel and let's go."

"Little buddy," Gleesty looked at me with his large watery eyes. "They aren't alive."

"I've been saying that for years," I said.

Gleesty turned around and lifted a wheezing man off the ground. His body was tied to one of my chairs. As he sat up straight, I watched his jaws expand and hungrily slam shut.

"Where did he come from?" I asked, turning to Mary. "This is totally illegal!"

"Watch," Mary petted the back of my head as she slowly backed away from Gleesty and his guest.

Gleesty grabbed a knife and advanced it on the man. He jabbed the man multiple times in the center of his chest with great precision. Blood spurted, but not as much as I expected. The man gasped quietly, completely unaware of what was happening to him. He raised his head up to me and growled. I jumped backwards and grabbed Mary's hand in terror and amazement.

I opened my mouth, "Zombies!" I could barely contain myself. "Why didn't you wake me up?! They were inside of my apartment?! Here?"

Gleesty looked at me with a very serious expression. "Listen, Mutt. I know we always talked about how great this would be, with the world needing, uh, a pruning and all, but we're all very worried. My family is out there, probably dead. Mary's too. John has been calling Wimsley without any luck. It's spreading fast. There isn't much time to think, so please just stay calm and help us out."

I agreed with Gleesty. I walked over to the couch John was sitting on and watched television for a moment. The event was on every channel. Footage in different states showing exactly what was happening outside. The walking dead looked up at the cameras in the helicopters. People were attempting to loot and being ambushed by dozens of zombies. Children were being separated by their limbs in the hoards. Thousands of citizens were trapped on bridges, trying to head west to escape the terror. It was only noon.

I stared at the screen. Zombies- slow, mindless, disease-ridden humans spreading their pestilence; devouring humans for the sake of extinction. It must have all happened in hours. Now I was pretty scared.

The camera panned towards buildings that looked familiar. It zoomed in closer on top of the structures. Owls were shown, sitting calmly, looking down at the carnage below with large grins from the rooftops. They looked responsible, but I didn't think this was their style. It didn't sit right with me. I was sure that they were just happy that we were suffering.

"Based on the time that attacks were first reported, we believe that the initial infestation occurred somewhere in central New Jersey. Nearly any wound can spread the virus almost instantly. It has also been reported that the victim will become one of these...monsters within four hours. The term Zombies, as they are dubbed by spiritual and cultural figures, appears to be the appropriate word for these creatures. This unnamed virus has no known origins just yet. However, if the zombie suffers a severe blow to the head, it will eliminate the threat, rendering the virus harmless. The Catholic Church has stated that the end-"

"Well," John said. "This got boring. I'm going to work."

Mary glared at John. "That's not funny. Our friends are probably dead out there."

"Whose friends?" He said. "Your little experiment? Gleesty doesn't care if his family dies. They believe in Valhalla!"

"No they fucking don't," Gleesty said. "I do."

"Calm down," John muttered. "Relax. The windows are pretty high up. I doubt any zombies will be able to reach us here. The door can hold. We have enough time to figure out a plan to get out of here."

"John," Gleesty said. "Zombies were already fucking in here! *You* had to open the door and see why a bunch of them were feasting on an eight-year-old boy!"

John laughed. "Oh, I forgot about that. I didn't know they were dangerous! I thought it was an interpretive dance ceremony. At 11 A.M."

"Alright, shut up," I said. I stood up from the couch and walked around for a few seconds. I lit a cigarette and continued my pacing. "Wimsley, Gleesty's family and Mary's specimen might still be alive. There is no reason we shouldn't try getting to their homes and helping them out. Hell, we need help too, and more manpower is what we could definitely use."

"Maybe I can use a jackhammer on this thing," John said. "Or a-"

Gleesty lifted John up by his collar and dropped him on the floor. "Not now. Don't start this. It's not funny."

John spat on a rotting hand. "Fuck you."

"Leave him alone," I said to Gleesty. "Can you blame him?" He sighed and apologized to John.

Mary wiped the sweat from her forehead and tried to remain calm. "Does anyone have a car or something?"

"Yeah," Gleesty said. "I have a garbage truck parked a few blocks away."

"It's probably long gone by now," John said. "Damn, a garbage truck would've been ideal."

"Hm, probably," Gleesty said. "I parked in a tow away zone. So how do we do it? We can run out there, arms flailing, hoping we can jump in a car before getting picked off."

"I'm hungry," Mary said. "Mutt, do you have any food?"

"Yeah, check the kitchen out. Uh, Glee, that's a terrible idea."

Mary walked to the kitchen. As she passed the restrained zombie, it let out a glass-shattering shriek. I clasped my hands over my ears and dropped to the floor.

The zombie fell backwards with the chair and stared at Mary. Mary panicked and shut her eyes as she flung her foot into the zombie's mouth. The sound of a jaw snapping relieved us as teeth and blood fired out of the infected cadaver's face and splattered on a nearby wall. The zombie went silent. It grunted with a puzzled look on his face. Then it started screaming again.

"Oh, fuck you!" Gleesty shouted. He lifted the chair that the zombie was fastened to and spiked it through my window. John shoved the lock box into his pocket and walked over to the new hole in the wall and examined the scenery.

John gasped. For the first time in my life, I heard John gasp; and I knew what was coming. "Crisis!" he shouted. "Crisis! Crisis!"

Gleesty rubbed his beard, "Hm, How many of them?"

"How many people are in the 'Last Supper' mural?" John blurted out with a cracking voice. "*That* many!"

"Are they able to pile up and get inside here?" Gleesty reached into his pockets for two leather gloves. I doubt he needed them; the calluses on his fists were incredibly thick. I remember being able to strike matches on them. John nodded at Gleesty and ran to the kitchen.

I ran to my bedroom and stuck my hand underneath the mattress. Feeling around for a few seconds, I finally found my M9 pistol. I checked the magazine, glanced at the single bullet inside and switched the safety off. I trotted back to the living room and stopped at the doorway. As I gathered my thoughts, I watched about a dozen zombies pile up and climb through the opening. Gleesty jumped right on it, killing each of them in a single blow to the head.

"Hah! It's like whack-a-mole!" he said, laughing hysterically.

I tucked the pistol inside of my pants. Gleesty seemed to have it under control anyway. Mary was sitting on the floor, looking very worried. I knelt down to assist her.

"What's wrong," I smiled. "You're acting like something terrible just happened."

Tears poured down her cheeks as she pet my face. She was choked up, barely able to speak. "His teeth got into my foot."

I closed my eyes and tilted my head down. I opened them back up and saw a tiny wound on the edge of her instep.

"I'm sorry," she said, breathing heavily. "I'm so fucking stupid. I'm so sorry." I grabbed her hand and pet it. I waited for Gleesty to finish his job.

The rest of the zombies were killed off. Gleesty turned around, covered in blood. His smile faded to a frown as he walked over to assess the situation. John came out of the bathroom with a hot towel, wrapping Mary's head with it.

"I'm going to become one of them, aren't I?" She said. "Oh my god."

"Calm down," John said. "Let's think for a second."

"You might as well just kill me and get it over with."

"No," I said. "What if there's a chance for a cure? You're going to be fine."

"That's extremely unlikely," she said. "You know as well as I do that I am probably fucked."

"I would rather keep you as one of them than kill you."

"What, like a pet?" Mary let out a fake giggle. The expression of fear was on her face. I was terrified of what was going to happen to her.

"Boys, come with me," John said. Gleesty and I followed him to my room. Mary sat there and muttered something about her clone.

"Okay, Mutt, you're probably right," he said. John's eyes suddenly changed. I noticed his concern for everything right after the scare he had. It worried me greatly. "We can't survive here, but she would be fine if we just handcuffed her to your bed or something."

"I don't want to leave her," I said. "It's not right."

"We have to at least search for Gleesty's parents. They do own a hospital nearby, as well as a shit load of other companies, right?"

Gleesty nodded with embarrassment. He was always a little ashamed with his parent's fortune and success. They have a famous bloodline and a well known history dealing with politics and medicine. Aside from hospitals, a great portion of their profits funded CERN, NASA, the Red Cross and a chunk of the government. The Goresmiths were the ones that introduced cloning, and were probably responsible for the war. Simply put, they run the show in this country. We knew he was the black sheep in his family, his two other brothers managed to take care of most of the business that their parents built from the ground up while he went out and did his own thing, whatever Gleesty does outside of our excursions. I respected Gleesty because of this. I hated his family and he knew it.

I looked at Gleesty. "You can call ove-"

Gleesty interrupted. "Already tried calling. They're all investigating this ordeal. No time to help us. They are expecting us over there, though."

"Fuck."

"No sense in phoning the cops either," John said. "Or drive to any hospitals. They'll probably just kill her themselves."

"So we get to their facilities, they supply us with whatever we need and take care of us. All set." John gave us a thumbs-up.

"So why not bring Mary with us?" I said.

"Chances are she will be shrieking to her zombie buddies to come over. We might as well just stick with leaving her here," John said. "We can't make it there in less than 4 hours. It's 5 towns over, and in this mess..."

"And Wimsley?" I said.

"I just saw him," Gleesty said.

"What? How?"

He pointed outside to his lifeless body. "There."

"So much for stopping at the bar."

"The best we can do is endure," John said." We keep Mary safe here, reach Gleesty's humble abode and then go wherever Mary's clone is."

"She's in a lab in Newark. Probably needed to refill her serum or something."

"Shit," John said. "They are in complete opposite directions. Franklin Lakes to Newark."

"We might as well try," Gleesty said. "We own that cloning lab. I'm sure we can get a chopper when we get to headquarters."

John nodded and headed towards the door. Just as he left the room, Gleesty grabbed him by the shoulder. "What's with you? You were a nihilistic auto-erotic asshole just 10 minutes ago."

John smiled. "Isn't it great?" He walked over to Mary.

"Uh, yeah," Gleesty scratched his head.

I grabbed Mary by the hand and picked her up. "Do you mind staying here until we find a cure and/or kill you?"

Mary laughed. "I heard your plan. Your walls are paper-thin." Mary hugged and kissed me. "It's all happening so fast. Can you at least handcuff me in the bathroom?"

The voices of zombies, like the rustling of leaves, surrounded the house. They were calm, but in ready to strike at any time. We gathered several items to help us survive our excursion: John, for some reason, removed the strings off of my wireless weed whacker and replaced them with kitchen knives. Watching the machine roar with the spinning blades made me feel a bit more secure, until I realized it was John holding it. Gleesty gathered cans of food and morphine, but not nearly enough to last us more than a week. With a handful of tools, a gun, and a road flare, we decided to leave Paterson and head for Franklin Lakes.

Mary transformed later on that night. We fastened and secured her the best we could so she wouldn't harm herself- we figured if there was a cure, we might as well keep her out of harm's way. Before she closed her eyes and woke up as a fiend, I promised that I would take care of her clone. Mary told me that she was to die for. I sure hoped so.

After we locked Mary down, we sat in the kitchen and planned a little more. I rested my back on the side of my refrigerator. Listening to the fan calmed me down. I could hear the occasional bone snap of a shin from a wandering zombie outside. Gleesty sat next to me, washing himself with a wet towel while whispering jokes. But his deep voice sounded nothing more than growls when he tried to speak quietly, so I could barely comprehend what he was saying. I was thankful for him trying to cheer me up, though.

John sneaked into the living room and watched the news for a little while longer. He heard that they broke out of the tri-state area through the sewers, avoiding the barricades of soldiers and sneaking up on them before taking them out. It was as if something was leading them through our defenses, they did not blindly wander. They also reported danger zones on a map with different colors. We were in the center of a big red dot. The plague must have started somewhere close by.

Eighth Chapter

A clone draft took place this morning. After much speculation, it was announced that recombinant clones, because of their abnormally slow blood flow, are not capable of falling victim to the illness. The virus travels slow enough for it to die before achieving its destination: the frontal lobes of the brain. I'm sure Mary would have been relieved to know this for the sake of her child. But therefore, all clones not injured or under repair must go out and fight along the borders of the red zones, where most have been ambushed and mauled to death. Real humans fight in the areas that are less threatening to their lives.

Scientists rushed to figure out the origins of the virus. They claimed that it was an advanced strain of a sexually transmitted disease. They are unsure how it mutated, but I can take a good guess.

Some coverage on the news also spoke about people turning to religion again. A few riots broke out in the west because people needed to "wake up, Judgment Day is nigh."

Gleesty nudged my side. "Are you ready?" He asked, strapping his gas mask on.

I shook my head. "Let me take one more look around," I wanted to make sure I grabbed everything that I would need in my backpack. After searching every room, with the exception of the bathroom, I managed to find one thing before I went back to Gleesty: A book John handed to me around the time Bill died. It was Bill's parting gift to me. On the cover it read, "A collection of Bill Struberies, And Other Various Cooking Recipes". Reading it would make time go by quicker. I have opened it up a handful of times out of curiosity. It was too strange for me; I had to lie to John and say that I read it all to make him happy.

I returned to Gleesty. He patted my back and nodded. John was leaning on the door that we blocked up earlier. He had arm and leg guards crafted from polyvinyl chloride pipes. John nodded at me, rolled the gas mask over his face and grabbed his kitchen knife weed whacker. Relying on him made me feel uneasy, but strangely exhilarated.

"We're going to walk, we're going to take it slow," Gleesty commanded. "If we get too tired, we may end up getting overpowered by 'em, then, who knows. We will keep quiet and try to not attract too many of them. From what we saw on the news, this epidemic doesn't seem to be under control by the military at all. There are more of them, and they look pretty fucking hungry."

"Okay," I said. "But do we rea-"

"GO!" Gleesty opened the door and rushed outside screaming, "fuck, fuck fuck!" John turned his weed whacker on and skipped merrily alongside with him, whistling a familiar tune. I followed in, the M9 in my left hand, and a knife in the other. I believe Gleesty carried two meat tenderizers and a flare gun.

As soon as I walked out of the door and turned to my left, I saw Gleesty and John hopping right to their mission, killing zombies with ease. Between the buildings and the street, there were about forty zombies, none of which seemed to acknowledge that they were being killed off with spinning metal blades and big metal instruments.

"Such fun! So-much-blood!" John said, laughing maniacally. Both of them made such a commotion.

Once all of them were dead, I whistled for their attention. They turned around, Gleesty giggling as he patted the blood off of his beard and mask.

"Uh, nice job," I said. "I'm glad you killed them all, but Franklin Lakes is this way, isn't it?"

They shrugged and marched forward, John sighing at me.

I walked a few feet behind my friends. While they went on their killing spree, they felt that I should carry all of the supplies; jesting about how much of a perfect pack mule I was.

Black feathers slowly rained down from the sky. I looked up past the light fog and saw thousands of crows inhabiting the sky. They flew in closer to the surface, their wings fluttering as their screeches grew louder. They gazed down with their sharp black eyes, scanning the area in curiosity on why their food was still moving. After several minutes of aimlessly flying, a few birds gave in and attacked the zombies. The rest of the flock swooped down. They pecked and tore off tiny pieces of flesh from the walking dead. Some of them collected scraps of clothing and made nests inside of their chest cavities. The zombies were too oblivious to notice the large birds feasting on them. The crows must be thrilled for traveling on and inside their food. Some grew so fat from the buffet that they actually dropped to the ground and died.

The birds were not the only party that followed the dead. The gnats were unbearable. They squeezed into my gas mask through the ear slots, then, buzzed around in front of my eyes before their little bodies were crushed between my eyelashes. I had to remove my headgear constantly to clean it out. The stench of metal gave me a headache. I lit a cigarette with a nearby car fire and crammed it into the air valve of my mask. It truly is a sad thing when smoking is healthier than breathing unfiltered air.

John whispered, "the swarm of whores." It gave me the chills.

I looked for a working car that we could steal at every street. Most of them were tipped over and smashed into buildings.

Gleesty chuckled after cracking every zombie on the head with his bludgeoning weapons. He was having all the fun as I sat in the back and sulked. He turned around and looked down at me. "Wish I was on shrooms," he yelled.

John let go of the trigger on his weed-whacker, "we'd trust you on shrooms?"

"Sure, why not?" he said as he advanced on a zombie cheerleader, taking her head clean off with his elbow. "Touchdown, bitch!"

"Very mature," John said. "Mutt, can you pick up anything that looks like a key along the way? I have this lock b-"

"I KNOW WHAT YOU HAVE!" I screamed.

"Cool, thanks!"

The furious white eyes of the enemy were the most intimidating thing about them. Their attempt to bite at us was pathetic. Swinging arms, mild groans and their half attempted chomps were nothing to worry about. Many of them hardly had any teeth. The PVC pipe armor that John made was very clever. I wondered how the zombies managed to be such a problem to the military.

We rested on top of a tipped over truck. Morphine and sandwiches were passed around. Canned bread, despite its poor reputation, is actually very good.

I glanced at the sky, trying to track down where the birds were coming from. I did a double take towards the buildings in front of me. Owls. I knew it was them when I caught sight of the torn black umbrellas.

One of them opened their mouths and began to speak. Her voice was soft and delicate. Her face was masked by a silk scarf. "Why is it the strange ones that manage to survive?" She said, laughing to herself.

Gleesty spat on one of the zombies circling us. "Was this your doing? And how's about a little help? Some booze, maybe?"

A group of the Owls laughed. "Why suppress the inevitable?" One of the male ones said. "You're only suffering much more than you should."

"Inevitable?" I asked.

"That's right," the female one squeaked. "A higher power is controlling this. Otherwise we animals would have built up a natural defense for this disease. We are dealing with a designer disease, lovely."

John sat quietly examining his lock box, hesitating to look up.

"I didn't think you over-educated Dadaists believed in a higher power," Gleesty yelled back.

The female Owl smiled and removed the scarf, revealing her surprisingly beautiful face. "This isn't just some extremely lucky outbreak. Listen to the dead in time."

The Owls hid behind the walls of the building. Gleesty was very annoyed with the whole situation. John was toying around with the lock box with his head down. He was hiding something.

"What's wrong with you, John?" I said.

"Nothing," He said. "Just thinking."

"About?" Gleesty asked.

"My uncle. If he mentioned anything about this."

"You can't be taking those loonies seriously! They're just trying to scare you."

John shrugged and laid down. "Probably. Yeah."

I stretched for a second and accidentally neighed. "Er, we better get going. If we rest too long our legs will grow stiff. Looks like the sun is setting too, so time isn't on our side."

John laughed. "Time is never on our side. We either have too much of it or too little of it."

I shrugged and swallowed a morphine tablet.

"Must have walked about two miles. By this time, we can get there by tomorrow night," Gleesty said.

"Sounds terrible," I said. "Let's find us a car."

Gleesty nodded. "What do we do once we find Mary's clone?"

I thought about this question a moment. "Well, your parents call the shots, right? We ask them to deport us to a safer continent, maybe a fallout vault, and just hang out."

"I can only hope," John said.

Gleesty shook his head. "I'd stay here."

John and I stared at him. He surely couldn't be serious.

"I believe in Valhalla," Gleesty joked. "Why run, right John?"

"You know, Gleesty, I respect that," John said.

Gleesty nodded. "My parents never approved of my ways. They wanted me to be a doctor like them, but fuck that. I want to fight and drink like my ancestors. I have plenty of brothers to take the family business."

John looked at him in admiration. "That's actually pretty sad."

Gleesty roared with a chuckle. He had to be intoxicated at this point. He snarled. The zombies glared at him. "I kind of like it up here. We might as well take our time."

"It's really not going to fit our schedule, and what if the zombies begin piling up on each other?" I said.

Gleesty shrugged. "Well, if those withered psychopaths up there are wrong, we have nothing to worry about."

I decided to take his advice and rest a little longer. I pulled Bill Strub's book out of my backpack and opened to a random page:

Bill Strub on SHC (Spontaneous Human Combustion)

It has been brought to my attention by my great grandfather on how the incredible phenomenon SHC can happen. Remarkably, thanks to the Wick Effect theory, the possibilities of humans bursting into flames is highly likely in America today. Fast foods, chronic depression, and abnormal sexual activities increases the chances drastically. As clothes being to soak up disgusting body grease from the human, it is very possible for static electricity to ignite the clothing and the human being. Alcohol may also be an ingredient during the process.

During my early work after I was kicked out of the university, I grew very fond of SHC and the deceased. If the dead body excretes all chemicals after all, there might actually be an adequate flash point in order for the subject to ignite.

The rest of the page was weathered; most of the words were rubbed away. I shut the book and closed my eyes, trying not to pay attention to the groaning flesh bags just a few feet beneath me.

I woke up a few minutes later to the sound of someone heaving. I stood up and saw Gleesty kneeling over the truck, vomiting blood. The sight of him almost turned my fur white.

"Gleesty!" I yelled. "John, what's wrong with him?" John said nothing. He sat up straight, meditating. He looked as tranquil as ever.

"Ahm aright," Gleesty said, spitting up the rest of the blood.

"Did they bite you?"

"No."

"Then why are you coughing up blood?"

"Not my blood," he said, laughing. "A few got up here while I was cleaning my mask. Caught me off guard."

I stared blankly at him.

"I'm fiiine. I just swallowed some blood when I broke one of their necks open." He sat back down and readjusted his gas mask. The air was cool and thin, good enough for us to breathe.

Gleesty tapped John's leg.

"Yes?" John replied.

"I was thinkin'," Gleesty said. "How's about I smash that lock box of yours open?"

"No."

"Why not? What if you never find a key? You might get killed out here."

John opened his eyes. "Inside it is probably something so delicate and precious that you would smash it to millions of pieces. I've been patient all these years, I'll wait for the key."

Gleesty shrugged and cleaned the blood off his face with a paper towel.

I finally took off my gas mask and looked around the renovated dystopia. The streets were damp with scattered intestines. It flowed down into the sewers where rats collected the floating body parts to feed their families. Buildings had the lives sucked out of them, they were now nothing more than gray, dull pieces of rock. Gunshots were heard coming from a few hundred feet behind us near black smoke lifting above large, red fires. The aura of the conflagrations lit up the darkening sky. Shattered glass was piled up next to twisted street signs.

Birds continued to pile up and feast on human remains. Stray dogs and cats popped their heads out of holes in walls and lapped up blood.

The smell was getting worse. Maybe I was the only one to notice, but Gleesty and John did not seem to realize the smell of rotting flesh yet. Perhaps they were used to it.

"Where do you think everyone went?" I asked.

"We killed most of *everyone*," John replied.

"Do you think they at least fought back before getting bitten?"

"What, them?" John stood up, his nose wrinkled as he threw up a middle finger at them. "These people?" He pointed at the handful of zombies that circled us. "They sit at home on their respirators and have morphine on the tap. They will sit in their beds with those tubes attached to them and not care if they lived or died. As long as they feel good, they will not lift a finger to protect their lives. Isn't this why you wanted this to happen? We had this requiem coming."

"John," I stood up and tried to calm him down. "Come on, I didn't mean it."

"Yes you fucking did."

"All life is precious. And perhaps you think too much without feeling."

"They weren't living. They were just waiting to die. And I think as much as I feel, otherwise I wouldn't dare say this."

I looked down at the zombies, "as hollow as they were alive."

"Dinner time!" Gleesty shouted, pulling out a bottle of vodka from a backpack. "Who wants to get drunk?"

We all decided to head out before it started to get too dark. Gleesty leaped off the truck, causing it to shake and almost knocking John and me off and into a pit of zombies. We adjusted, looked down to see Gleesty releasing powerful blows to each enemy. His beard was covered in so much blood that it dried and hardened to a fine point. I warned him about cutting it before it got out of hand. He strongly disagreed with the idea, hiding his flare gun in his mammoth-like facial hair.

"You could paint me a picture with that fucking thing. Be careful, don't stab yourself."

"Dude," Gleesty yelled. "I have like, 10,000 HP."

Most of the stores we passed were already looted. The next street after the truck we rested on had a weapon shop. The doors were locked, except for one window, which had the bars pried off.

I was handed the weed whacker, but did not get to use it. John went inside first, since he was the skinniest one without physical abnormalities. He walked around quietly and unlocked the door for us.

"No hope here," he said. "Mostly everything is gone."

We all shrugged and sat around, scanning for any lucky finds. I managed to find a box of bullets for my gun. An empty box. John let out a wail. "Yeah!" He screamed, picking up a samurai sword. "I'm a fucking ronin!"

His excitement was awkward for him, especially for such a useless find. "It's crap, John."

"What do you mean?" He said. "It's a sword; you're just saying that because you have a gun."

"Leave it alone and find something better, buddy," Gleesty said. "Slicing weapons aren't too great for this type of battle, unless you're real strong. It'll wear down easily and it requires a lot of effort to slice their heads off. And if it gets stuck, you're fucked."

"Eh," he said, lobbing the sword at me, nearly slicing my hoof. "Hang on to it just in case. It still looks cool. Real samurai swords are hard to come by."

"Stick with your whirling blades, you sick bastard." Gleesty said. John grabbed the weed whacker from my hands.

I examined the blade. It was crafted with Damascus steel, and was very well balanced. I picked the sheath up from the counter and strapped it to my back. I felt cool.

Gleesty turned the television on that was adjusted in a corner of the room. The news was on almost every available channel. We tuned in to one that had very little static. It was a talk show. The captions shown on the bottom screen made our jaws drop: *I'm a clone that's still screwing my zombie parent.*

"Why?" Glee muttered.

A white male in his mid-thirties sat on the chair, smiling to himself. The camera panned out to the crowd, shocked at his behavior. Some hissed, some booed, and others just shook their heads. The talk show host walked towards the guest and stuck his microphone near his face.

"So, um, tell me Mr. Charles, why are you doing this?" The talk show host said. I think his name was Theodore.

"I still love him," the man in the chair said. The crowd roared with disgust. The workers of the show stood up and tried to ease the audience. *"I called the doctor and told him about the man that cloned me. He was just bitten by a zombie while coming home from work. At first I freaked out about the situation- that he was going to... transform. I then asked the doctor if I could catch this disease through intercourse. He hung up the phone."*

"And, we all found out on the news that clones are immune..." Theodore said.

Charles nodded with a smile. *"Like most illnesses for clones, we are immune. Of course, I can't be the receiver anymore because rigor mortis has settled, but we are working on trying to figure out how to get it up at all times."*

"Does he bite?"

Charles laughed and winked. *"He always did."*

John stood up and changed the channel before I could release my fit of rage. There was an infomercial of a zombie cure elixir for five hundred dollars. I grabbed the sword and swung at the screen, knocking it off the wall. Humans were all still influenced by greed. I stared at the T.V. as it plunged to the ground, shattering with a loud crash. Shards of glass and plastic surrounded my hooves; sparks jumped up and seared some of my fur. I stared angrily down at the wreckage. A sardonic smile graced my face.

"Mutt," John said. "You look delightfully morbid. I bet it's the sword."

We all gathered at a table to rest once more. I turned a radio on that was sitting next to us. Gleesty stood up and headed towards a bathroom.

"Our country, once upon a time, had balls," I said. "Where's that nuclear boot to stamp us all out?"

"Heh," John kindly acknowledged me as he listened carefully to the radio.

Thanksgiving is almost here!

John closed his eyes and stretched for a few seconds. "Now that's my kind of genocide." He opened them back up and revealed his warm, watery eyes. They were same kind of eyes that I caught a glimpse of when Mary was bitten. John either has a split personality or very strange mood swings.

The radio went to static. I took the cable from the television and started to adjust it to the radio. This setting was introduced when the fog first appeared. The radio has a fully-digital function for times when the fog is too thick.

"Mary turning into a zombie was the single moment in your life where you felt free."

"Excuse me?" I said.

"Think about it. She drove you into a downward spiral. Mary slept with you, got you addicted on a few terrible substances, then she went out of her way to sleep with her clone. You tried to get over her, but you couldn't, not with that shit in your veins. The only way she could escape your mind is if she was destroyed.

"You hope this clone of hers isn't as twisted as her parent. You want to find her to have the love you had with Mary, and have the happiness you never had with her."

I felt ashamed at what he was telling me. In a way, he was right. It is very clear what I wanted all along. I looked straight at John and expected a disgusted face. It was not there. The same warm, loving eyes were still attached to his head.

"I don't blame you." He said.

We both smiled. Gleesty walked back into the room, smelling a little bit more sanitary. He washed the blood off his face and conditioned his beard. "We might as well sleep here tonight, but we're getting up early tomorrow and headin' straight for the Goresmith Facilities. I gave my family a call, everything over there is under control. They're already working for a cure!"

"Impressive," John said.

"Aye. Zombies all over the place, though. We have a great defense system built around all of our buildings. Oh, and more states are reporting sightings. They think the virus is spontaneously showing up somehow. Might be in the water system."

After a few moments, the radio cleared up and a news bulletin was announced.

The time is 8:34 P.M. This is an emergency bulletin. Zombies have appeared to act much more aggressive than the first sightings. It appears that the bodies are finally growing out of rigor mortis and will eventually move as quickly as an ordinary human. Studies have shown that because of the atmospheric condition, zombies can digest the debris in order to survive. There have hardly been any signs of decomposition from the test subjects. We now know that the virus is restraining any bacteria, preventing the bodies to decompose for at least 5 years.

"Oh shit," Gleesty yelled. "They don't rot?"

This just in! The government has recalled all National Guard units that set foot on New Jersey in fear they may also become infected. All current residents in New Jersey must wait until further notice for another evacuation to occur at your local firehouse or refuge center.

"Well, that's not good," I said.

My friends kept quiet.

"I guess this was my fault. If I didn't let Mary over, we probably would have enough time to get out of this mess. I wish I never met her."

Gleesty spoke up. "Don't say that."

"That's a pretty silly thing to say," John said. "If you never met Mary, you probably would never have had the opportunity to meet this gentle, now raging, giant next to us."

Ninth Chapter

Sometime after my parents died, I managed to get a job as a crematory operator. I was lucky enough for Bill to let me stay over his house with John. Sometimes Mary came over to drug me up. John greatly disliked this and often told Bill to handle the situation without murdering us. My last conversation with Mr. Strub was like any other ordinary chat with him. After those final words, he disappeared.

"Do you think I am outrageous?" Bill Strub asked.

"Compared to everyone else this world? No. I hope I don't sound pretentious with that answer, sir." I said.

"Compared to all the other smart-ass kids your age? Not at all. I was like that too, once.

"When I was your age, Pluto was still a fucking planet. I was so shallow back then. I used to masturbate to the golden ratio in my teen years. I felt beauty and math belonged together. But math equally belongs with the ugly as well. There is a place for everyone in math."

"Why are you telling me this?"

"Because it's arbitrary, and the only way I would ever turn myself inside-out is if I dissect my thoughts into an abstract state and rebuild my body from the ground up.

"Did I ever tell you that I am the only human to ever remember his birth? It's true. And I plan on leaving this world the same way I got here- naked, bloody and furious."

"You are very odd."

"The odd are superior in this world. They overpower the even, especially in pi!"

"Excuse me?"

"Within, let's say, six billion decimals of pi, the odd digits occur 600,166,527 times more than even digits. So therefore, even in math we see the odd ones more. Why do you think we have shittier days more than better days? Go ask the fucking calculator.

"And get off that shit."

"What? Junk?"

"Yeah. I don't want you living here if you will keep at it. The last thing I need is a pet with a nasty habit."

A few hours passed and John found me convulsing in my room with a syringe still in my arm. In fear that his house may be condemned if he called the police over, this panicking John drove me into an animal hospital, which sent me to a human hospital that saved my life. Bill was not home at the time, and I am glad too. He would have just had me stuffed.

Many of my old friends, who I no longer speak to, asked me why I got into such a nasty habit. It was Mary who started it all. Mary got me into heroin when we first met. Just to entertain herself. She said it was just as fun as watching her cat flip out on PCP. The addiction started with a few shots once or twice a week after we slept together. During this time her clone was in the process of being created, so I was around for kicks until her masterpiece was finished. The more I shot junk, the less I saw of her. John would watch my room closely from the outside, waiting for her to leave. Once she left our house, John would go into my room and eye me up and down.

He does two things in his life if he is not working at the bar: watch me suffer and meditate. At a young age, he managed to earn his master's degree in physics and mechanical engineering. I am not sure why he chose to become a bartender.

I was sent to a rehabilitation center in New Jersey after the incident. Bill refused to even keep me in his house if I returned; I had to move once I was released from the place. It turned out that I suffered a heart attack and an overdose at the same time. My mutated donkey heart is too large for a drug like heroin. Some animals just can't handle junk.

Goresmith Care Center, owned by Gleesty's family is where I resided for two months. There are four wings on every floor. I sat in the center of the second floor, next to the nurses and looked down all day. I memorized nearly all 400 residents just by their footsteps. I was feared by the old and the retired on the first floor, hated by the addicts on the second, and revered by the mentally unstable on the third. It was an all around terrible place to be in just because of the way people looked at me; not including the ex-professors with long fingers, the nurses with missing teeth, or the single-breasted models with missing feet. John visited often, which strangely enough kept me sane.

The first week was nothing but sleep. I woke up at 8 A.M. every day, something I have not done in years. It wasn't an alarm clock that woke me up, or the nurses. It was the morning shit that the elders took in the first floor of the place. It was always at eight, on the dot, with every resident. The smell was too outstanding not to notice and it lingered for over an hour.

I got used to the smell by the second week, only to experience something far worse. I was jumped by a crack addict and a war veteran. The crackhead hit me in the back of the head with a very large blunt instrument as the veteran attempted to tear my ears off. No more than two seconds later, I kicked with my leg, nailing my hoof through one of the men's shoulders, who bled to death a few minutes afterward. The other continued to smash the front of my face into the floor yelling at the back of my head all the while until the security guard lifted him off of my back and threw him into the other bloodied attacker. I looked at his name tag, which read a very unusual name: Gleesty.

He picked me up off of the floor and took me to get stitched up for five hours. I suffered from a large gash on the back of my head and on my forehead along with a broken nose.

"What's yer name, little donkey man?" he asked.

"Mutt."

"Charmed. Heard a lot about you upstairs. They preach about ya, sayin' you are their donkey-headed savior. Some also call you Set- an Egyptian god or some shit like that."

"Wish it was like that down here."

"There's gotta be Hell somewhere. Well, what are ya here for? You can't just be here for being too ugly."

I laughed. "Heroin. Had a big problem with it."

"Ah. And do you plan on quitting when you leave this place?"

"Nope."

"Once a junkie always a junkie. O.D.?"

"Yep, and a heart attack." I rubbed my chest and shrugged at the giant. He squirmed involuntarily and rubbed his beard.

"You certainly don't look too old."

"Hey, I'm probably younger than you!"

"I'm seventeen."

I examined his figure-absolutely gigantic for his age. Even his facial hair was sprouting out of his face like a middle-aged man. "Close enough."

"Heart attack at our age, you're worryin' me, little buddy."

"Only with my heart condition. I'll be back on something when I leave this place. Probably not tar, maybe something that can give me the same mental state but keep my blood pressure up."

"I wish you luck."

I nodded. "And what's a mammoth-like neanderthal doing at a place like this?"

"I'm Gleesty. My family runs this place, along with other human 'resource' centers. One of my brothers took control of this building; he was kind enough to let me work here."

"So, you're the flusher?"

"I prefer the term runt. Whatever, I'm cool with it. The upper-class is not my way of life. Too perfect. No problems, no satisfaction."

"No denial."

He let out another laugh, scaring the shit out of the other patients as we walked out of the tiny clinic.

"So why are you so, uh," I tried to not offend him. Even though he didn't seem like a person that would attack me, I felt insecure after the initial beating.

"Large?" he smiled.

"Yeah."

"Genetics, apparently. My family always teases me. Sometimes they say I'm a mutant, sometimes they say I derived from Vikings." I laughed in disbelief. "I know," he said. "My family does have a legacy that not too many care to know about. I mean, I do love mead!"

"I guess I believe it. Get into a lot of fights?"

"Do you really think people would fight me?"

"I'm sure you've come across people your size before."

Gleesty lifted up his shirt, revealing a forest of body hair. He reached for a group of long, red hairs next to his ribs and ripped out a handful. Blood dripped between his fingers and down into his pants. He dropped his shirt and blew the hairs out of his hand.

"Okay," I said. "What the fuck was the point of that?"

He laughed and nodded. "I have to get going, I'll see you around."

The following day I sat in the same spot and looked down listening to footsteps and wheelchair squeaks. I heard John walk over and I looked up, the blank expression never leaving his face.

"You deserve it after all of this," he said, smiling.

I nodded with a frown.

"Your face makes me want to call security."

"Okay," I put my hand up to shield his insults from my face. "Stop."

"So what happened?"

"They don't take too kindly to my type."

"Sounds like a morality issue. They probably aren't used to seeing freaks such as yourself in a clinic like this, and you mutants did only start showing up this generation."

There was a pause as I gazed into John's eyes for a few seconds. "Will you cut the pseudo anthropocentric bullshit and get me some water?" He shrugged and put a dollar into the vending machine, then pressed a button for a soda. He picked it up and handed it to me.

"I can't stand soda, John."

"Just have some sugar. Your nurse told me you've had nothing but bread."

I grunted.

"Perhaps you would care for a salt-lick?"

"Asshole, just give it."

John smiled as he handed me the soda. He reached into his coat pocket and pulled out a stack of papers and put them into my other hand.

"What's this?"

I looked down, read one of the titles and sighed.

The Telekinetic Exoskeleton

"Bill Strub essays! Your favorite! Includes my favorites: The Pinnacle of Quantum Alchemy, Euphoria After Agony, Why We Yearn To Destroy Ourselves, The Dada Alphabet, and the Solar Blender!"

"How is Bill doing anyway?"

"Just fine, he misses you."

I shrugged. "Um, I don't know about reading this, John, but I'm trying to get cured here, not become a bigger threat to, urh, all of existence."

"But what's existing without the non-existing? We are only here to take a break from nothing, and sometimes you just cannot wait to go back into non-existing. So like me and my uncle, we do nothing but dream for the part in life where and when you cannot dream!"

"One question."

"Hm?"

"Why did you save me? Isn't that a contradiction?"

"Well, I don't have any friends."

"I wonder why."

"No need to get personal."

"You praise, no. You *worship* the ideal to shatter reality and everything living, but you cannot live without trifling things such as friendship?"

"Yep. We've gone over this many times."

"We have?"

"Yeah, you just were too intoxicated to remember. I kept slipping all these weird chemicals and agents in your drinks when you lived with me."

I fired the soda out of my mouth and stood up from the chair, "You what?!"

"You fascinate me; you fuzzy, humanistic, poor excuse for a mammal you!"

"Is that why you gave me a soda instead of water?!" I was ready to scream for security. I could not believe he would pull that on me.

"Well, yeah. The juices of the peyote taste so bitter. Oh, you're going to feel like shit for a few hours." John backed up into the fire exit and ran off. Before the door shut by itself, I heard him yell, "Hope-you-don't-get-too-angry-write-down-your-dreams-seeya-soon!"

John visited me often, but the visits were very short. After weeks, I warmed up to every resident there. Once I peeled off their crusty, flaky exterior, I found every single one of them had a story to tell similar to mine. They were always sad, they always wanted to leave. They had no place to go but this place. I saw a little bit of my parents in them.

I spoke to Gleesty every other day. He told me about his family and why he chose to live with an average job, despite his appearance. For kicks, I gave Gleesty Mr. Strub's essays once I trusted him enough. He was probably the only person I ever met without any mental problems. I thought maybe I could change that. Five days later and still no sight of John nor Gleesty. On the sixth day, almost five weeks in, John arrived.

"Hey," he said. "I just felt I should come clean with my experiments for once. Not even sure why I did them. I guess my uncle rubbed off on me."

"I'm too fucking bored to be angry," I said. "But an apology would be good right about now."

He looked up at the ceiling. "Nah."

"I'm not surprised."

"Hey, Mutt, listen. I have some bad news. Bill is dead."

"Excuse me?"

"He's gone. Dead. Just gone. We were meditating and he just went poof."

"Poof?"

"Yes, I think it was part of one of his experiments. Anyway, I'm not too worked up about it, you shouldn't be either. The main thing is that he is gone and he still doesn't want you living with me."

"John, wait a second. Bill Strub disappeared. You saw him die?"

"Well, no. This gas was on and really messed me up. I woke up and he left this death memoir with this lock box. There's something hidden in this that he wants me to figure out to open."

"Like a puzzle box?"

"Yeah, only I need to find a key to open it, which could be anything."

"Jesus Christ, John. I, you. I-I really don't know what to say. I'm so-"

"No, don't be sorry. Please, life goes on."

"Alright, buddy. Wait, he can't evaporate, that doesn't make sense! Did you kill him?"

John paid no attention to what I was saying. "I, however, do have good news."

"You're going to put me to sleep?"

"Nah, you've had enough needles in you. Which reminds me, why inject?"

"Hm?"

"It's pure enough to snort or eat it..."

"Might be masochism. I just love the part when the needle breaks through. Any other way looks boring. I like style."

"Shitty, but okay. Anyway," He pulled out a cigarette from his pocket and lit it inside the place. A nurse kindly asked him to put it out. John bit the filter off and spit it at her and continued smoking, the nurse walked away furious. "That crematory job you had, I told your boss that you have a heart condition, I didn't bother mentioning drugs. They will gladly give your job back once you get out of here."

"Best news I've heard in a long time. Did you hear that, everyone?!" I stood up and glanced at the brain dead patients staring at the ceiling in the middle of the hallway from their wheelchairs. "I get to burn you all once you die!"

John giggled lightly.

I nodded and sat back down.

"Well, how are you, anyway? I noticed your wounds are much better."

"Oh, John, if I was any better, I'd be dead."

"You're the fuck of England," he said, sharing a laugh. He handed me the cigarette for a drag as he blew into a fire alarm.

"The people here warmed up though, well, everyone except for some old war veterans. They don't think I belong here."

"I don't either."

"No, I mean on Earth."

"Yeah, I don't either."

I laughed. "The rehab folks don't push me aside in the cafeteria line anymore."

John laughed. I stood up again and pulled out a piece of paper. John waited impatiently.

"What's that?"

"A resident from the third floor drew me a picture." I handed it to him; he scanned every inch of the picture as he laughed hysterically. It was a drawing of Satan flying a crucifix kite that Jesus was attached to.

"Oh gosh, old king Bill would have loved this. Probably show it off to his owly friends."

"That always bothered me. Why would a mathematician, or scientist, or whatever he is, hang out with a bunch of art freaks?"

"Bill never believed in walls."

"What?"

"Everything should be combined with everything. There should be no boundaries. That way, possibilities are endless. All thoughts and entities should make crazy eights, chasing each other in a perpetual flow of interest. That way any vision is possible."

"Huh?"

"Mutual annihilation!"

"John, please."

"Why should art and science be separate? You cannot understand something without understanding everything about it, every field that it can fit in; whether it be a block of wood or a building; so much information can be learned as it just--branches out. It's ignorant to think you know everything about a hammer when you know nothing about the nail."

"Gotcha."

"You're just going to shake your head an-"

"No, actually, I agree for the first time."

John smiled.

"And this mutual annihilation thing is just your example of the thinking process?"

"Yep," John danced as his twirled his fingers in a circular motion. "The pattern of thought is like the snake eating itself."

"That's really weird."

"No-you."

"Yeah, it is. Your uncle believed in the infinite spiral, not a perpetual circle."

"The snake starts with the thinnest part of its body, then, becomes thicker."

Now he was just trying to confuse me. I decided not to play along. "Alright, I see."

John walked to the trashcan and threw his cigarette away. He walked into a resident's room and stole a chair to sit next to me. I thought about Bill for a second, and what John just told me about his strange death. Perhaps the Owls were part of it? It made me uncomfortably curious.

"What are the Owls like?" I said.

John stayed silent.

"He's brought you around, hasn't he?"

John nodded. "Yeah, they don't like me."

"Why not?"

"I'm too young to understand, but I understand them perfectly. They think I'm arrogant."

"They are threatened by how advanced in absurdism you are?"

"Yeah, uncle taught me everything. But I still want answers to the big questions. He had them. I have this now, though. I think I'm almost ready." He finally showed me the lock box. "Inside contains all of the answers. Imagine that. All the secrets, and I might even know where he went after earth.'" John's eyes sparkled with anticipation.

"Have you tried his urethra rods?"

"Yeah, nothing fits. I tried all 42 of them."

"Just break it open."

"No. What if the box itself is the answer? Besides, I'm not going to cheat to find my answers. That's ugly. Cheating is ugly. Did I mention how ugly you are, Mutt?"

"Just trying to blend in with my surroundings." I felt someone grope my back and quickly move to my shoulder. It squeezed, cracking that portion of my body and releasing.

"Hey, kid," Gleesty said, nodding to John.

The initial grab shocked me enough to make my voice squeak. "Ay, Gleesty. Haven't seen you in a few days, thought you hated me."

"Nah, you keep it interesting."

"I suppose. This is John."

John looked up at him and gazed into his eyes.

"That nurse told me about a smoking problem. Figured it was going on here." Gleesty squinted at John.

"No problem."

Gleesty nodded, flaring his nostrils and relaxed after a smile spread across his face.

"You ever hear a death rattle?"

"Death what?" Gleesty scratched his nose. "Is that a videogame?"

"Rattle. The last breath *out* when a person passes."

Gleesty stayed silent with an appalled look on his face.

I elbowed Gleesty's side. "No need to answer him. It's his defense mechanism. He has to constantly weird people out."

Gleesty went back to a smile, not as big as the original, but enough to show he understood. "I've dealt with plenty of sociopaths. No problem." John smiled back. "I've seen plenty of old-timers die. It's not unusual here, the turnover rate is pathetic. But the strangest thing that ever came over me was the passing of a hag named Ann Marie. A real serious chain smoker, she had more cigarettes in her mouth at the same time than teeth. So one day it was finally her time. She toppled over her chair outside during her smoke break, gasping desperately, obviously a heart-attack. I ran over and gently placed my hand near her neck, watching her brown eyes rolling up into her head. When all I saw was white, she exhaled a stream of smoke."

"Wait, wait," John said. "You let them smoke outside in this fog?"

"No, they have their outside breaks on this roof, now shut up. When she breathed out, I watched the smoke climb out her throat, first a hand, then two arms. The arms grabbed my neck as the rest of her gray soul illuminated by smoke hoisted itself out of its shell. And that gurgle, so damn subtle. Scary shit." John's eyes glistened, waiting for more.

Gleesty searched his back pocket and revealed to me Bill's essays. "Reminds me. Weird *and* scary shit."

John's eyes took over the sockets, his mouth's smile sliced through his face, "my uncles writings! You like?"

"This explains a lot about you."

"He just passed away."

"I'm sorry to hear that, mate. I hope you're not too torn up about it. Death is a ter-"

"Yeah, so, any more stories, Gleesty?"

John's lack of care startled Gleesty. "I'd be one sick bastard to share them with you," he said as he kindly handed John the stack of papers with a smile. Gleesty turned around and stepped inside of an elevator, his smile now wide and creepy. He gave a wink before the elevator doors closed.

"So Mutt, do you like this place?"

"No."

"Why?"

"Because the people you like die, and the people you don't like don't die."

Tenth Chapter

Gleesty and I sat in the same spot for hours just listening to the radio. We decided to spend the night at the gun shop. I have been debating on taking the final morphine tablet the entire time. I have not had a true hit since Mary came over last night. John was gone; he locked himself in the basement of the gun shop for a solid three hours. We have heard nothing but drilling and welding and laughing the entire time.

I sat and watched Gleesty drink as we shared small talk. It took him an incredibly long time to get drunk. He ransacked the entire building for booze and drank at least two handles of vodka by himself. In fact, I do not recall him not drinking this entire time. Minutes after the bottles of vodka, he found the only remaining bottle of beer; one without a twist-top. Bottle opener-less, my friend pried the top off with his bare hand. If only the military cloned beasts like this man.

The clones that have been drafted thus far have been able to slow down the zombies, but not enough to keep them in New Jersey, so says the radio. The military is being forced not to shoot unless it is absolutely necessary. They admitted today that they will try to contain the ill humans within fences and walls, this won't work. They can only fire when attacked. The zombies are moving faster now. They have now spread through Pennsylvania, New York, and halfway into Delaware already. The government's long term plan is to continue the quarantine until they get confirmation to firebomb selected locations. All I really cared about was this tiny pill.

Gleesty grunted. "When's he comin' out?"

"I don't know. You can try pulling that door open."

"He'll just get pissed off and whine."

"Fine, I'll go check."

I got up from my stool and pounded on the basement door, waiting for a response. Nothing. I kicked at it with my hoof until the bottom of the door splintered. Finally, John shouted.

"Yeah?!"

"Will you just get up here and tell us what the fuck you are doing?"

"I'm done!"

"Done? "

"Yeah, I've been done a half hour ago."

"So, why don't you come up?"

John did a loud sigh and stomped up the stairs. "I've been trying to open up this fucking lock box for the last half hour with magnets and worms!" John opened the door, gasping for breath. His face was red and he looked completely exhausted. John was pulling up a large black bag on a hand truck.

"Worms?" Gleesty said.

"Yeah, the bottom of the food chain. I think I need to figure out the riddle to Bill's lock box. If I get the riddle, I can figure out the key. If I get the key, I open it. It's made out of stone, so no magnet can pry it open. So I figured the lowest animal in the world might be able to unlock the world's greatest mystery; perhaps that was the key. Well, unless there is no riddle. Blast."

"Good concept."

"Yeah, but not good enough, apparently."

"What happened to the worm?" I said.

"I shoved it in halfway, and it refuses to go in any further. I still don't even know how deep this keyhole is."

"In time, John," Gleesty muttered. "What do you have in the bag?"

John's frown turned into a big grin. "My uncle would be so proud of me. I still am brilliant."

"It can't beat the bladed weed whacker," Gleesty laughed.

"Well, I have a few new weapons, two are for you." John unzipped the smaller pouch of the bag and pulled out two massive heavy duty hammer tackers.

"What the fuck is that?" Gleesty said.

"Staplers." John said. "Well, hammer tackers. Carpenters use them to put stuff up with staples. I modified these to add a bigger kick with pistons, and extended the handle for you just in case."

Gleesty picked one up and slammed it at the door. The staple exploded, blowing a nickel-sized hole through it. "My Forseti, yes." His eyes glistened. "Yes, this will do."

John handed him three boxes of staplers. "You can kill about 500 of them."

"Sold."

"And what about me?" I said.

"You're the jackass, we went over this already."

"Like we even need the supplies," I pouted. "As soon as we find a car we can drive to Goresmith Headquarters in no less than a half hour."

"Oh fine," John said. He walked to the weed whacker that was charging and yanked it off the socket. "It's good for another five hours. Use it as long as you hang on to that sexy katana."

I smiled for the first time on the adventure.

"What about you, John?" Gleesty said.

"Well, I'm going to get us out of here with my weapon. Inside this bag is the greatest thing I ever created.

My Magnum Opus. It's even better than *The Periodic Table of Elements Hopscotch!*"

"Go on."

John pulled out of the bag what looked like to be a very large mortar cannon made out of iron.

"We're using pipe bombs?" I said.

"Nope."

"Lasers?" Gleesty said.

"Gay. I call it the slushgutter."

"Sounds terribly lame."

"Well, yeah. The zombie masses are thickening up ahead. So I made this to plow through the wall of flesh. It's a one-time use weapon. I built it out of the welding machine and some other interesting things I found down there. It's really heavy."

"You're going to use it once and then what?"

"You don't get it. We only *need* to use it once. At the base of this cast-iron tube is a time-released positive magnetic charge. The large metal rocket has a negative charge. It took me a good hour just to contain the weapon at the base of this metal tube. We only have about ten minutes before the timer goes off."

"Then we die?"

"Maybe. The charge will then go to negative. The 'bullet' inside this thing is a very powerful magnet. Think of it as a Gaussian gun. A big one! Whee! They had neodymium down in the basement! Can you imagine that?! Anyway, I drilled at the bottom of it and was able to contain an extremely expensive power cell inside. The electrons are just *screaming* to dismantle the area. I had to build a tiny neutralizing vacuum shell inside so it does not kill us all prematurely."

"Okay," I said. "I understand the concept, but what I don't understand is how you did this inside of a gunsmith's basement and why you didn't tell us. We would have gladly moved to another building."

"If I'm going down, you two go with me. So I am going to set it up and aim it down Main Street. Hopefully, with the tiny wings I added to this magnetic bullet, it should fire down a good half of a mile. It'll attract everything to it like a horizontal tornado of metal, shredding everything in its path."

Our eyes twisted in disbelief. "Bullshit."

"Well, we don't have a lot of time to do this. Main Street is a street over and I need Gleesty to carry it."

"John, should I take my last morphine tablet?"

"Celebrate! It's going to be one fuck of a show."

I looked around the place to prepare for the move. I decided not to take the radio; not too many exciting things were being discussed anyway. Gleesty opened the door to inspect his enemies. The zombies have been rather quiet the last hour.

Then, they moaned. John and I thought that they were charging at Gleesty. They screamed in a single monotonous chant. Calm and soothing at first, then like a thunderstorm. The nation heard the death rattle of the Earth. The anchormen on the radio were no longer silent. It was easy to tell how nervous they were when they spoke.

UUUUUHHHHNNNNNN-
WWWWWAAAHHHHHHRRRRRR

I was too sober to deal with the maleficent chanting burped up by the thousands of plagued humans. A chill ran down my spine. I expected doom to end our chronic remorse at any second. The shrieking scared me so much that I dropped the pill, losing it under the table.

Gleesty's jaw shook as well. "Oh my. They certainly caught our attention."

John tried to speak, but all his lips did was word out "Bill."

The radio played static for the time being. It was difficult to find out what was going on, and we were too scared to look outside.

"Th-" John gasped. His eyes were tearing as he tried to swallow. "There's a television in the basement."

We rushed down the stairs, plugged the television in and waited for picture. We skimmed for a good shot of the chaos. Helicopters and satellites zoomed in on the walking dead, trying to figure out what they were trying to communicate to humans. They continued their attempt to word out their message with their stiff jaws. The zombies, thousands of them, looked down at the ground. The birds and insects crawling on them scattered.

The event was taking place everywhere; cameras from other states shared their footage. The zombies were found kneeling on the concrete pavement. Others stood on cars; many were also kicking into the sands on shorelines. Suddenly, the cameras panned out to the Owls once again. They joined in on the demonic hum. They all gathered on the rooftops, on their knees, their mouths flaring wide open. They repeatedly raised their arms into the air and lowered them. Their fingers wiggling slowly as if they were putting on a puppet show.

"Guys, did we deserve this?" Gleesty mumbled to us.

Then, the evil stopped moving. They went back to their silence. The Owls sat on their roofs and observed patiently. Then, in an eerie organized manor, the thousands of plagued humans tried to tell us what was on their minds in a different way. Every 20 feet a mass of zombies separated into large circles in streets, on beaches and rooftops.

More live footage was being broadcast. Zombies were grinding their hands on concrete walls, using their blood as ink, until their limbs were nothing more than little stubs. They scrawled giant red letters while wheezing uncontrollably.

More footage, but this time on the beaches. They pulled out their insides and placed their intestines in mounds of sand. The letters in the trenches, disoriented and cryptic, turned a dark, outstanding red.

There was not a single reporter that kept their sanity. They all went hysterical, crying to their families live on camera.

And when the birds flew back down for an afternoon snack, the zombies grabbed a hold of the flying critters. Every bird that was caught was mutilated and flung onto the walls and into the sands to form stronger, bolder letters. The cameras cut again, to people like us trapped on rooftops all over New Jersey and New York. The rust fog was so high in some places it just consumed buildings. It was heartbreaking to see so many suffer from so much.

In each of the crowds there was a different word. Several of the undead would look up at the helicopters and smile, revealing their crusty yellow teeth. Some cameramen in helicopters were so shocked by this that they jumped off to end it.

There were various satellite screen-shots of the words these soldiers of the apocalypse wrote down. The three of us tried to decipher the message; as well as anyone else watching.

Then, they all took a deep breath and roared like angry dogs. Now their voices were clear and comprehensible.

They shall hunger no more, neither thirst any more;
neither shall the sun light on them, nor any heat.

It was a quote from the Book of Revelations. The message was now clear. The Owls were true with their words.

They continued their monotonous phrase. John had a smirk on his face, "well, there's the answer to Agnostics." Gleesty and I breathed in heavily. John turned away from the television and nodded at us. We ran upstairs to look out the window.

And I saw an angel standing in the sun; and he cried with a loud voice, saying to all the fowls that fly in the midst of heaven, Come and gather yourselves together unto the supper of the great Him.

We saw Owls on their perches slow dancing. John ordered Gleesty to prepare his weapon.

The radio was still on. "Oh my God, oh my God," was heard over the news anchormen. "The end is nigh!" The broadcast was then overwhelmed with static.

"Well," Gleesty said. "We *did* ask for it."

I stayed silent. John's smirk never left his face. He was hiding his true emotions, his eyes looked worried. "We can survive."

"Bullshit."

"No, I can explain some things, but there really is no time." John glanced at his weapon of mass destruction. "Let me just say that Bill didn't teach me some things for nothing. There is a reason the Owls hated me and wanted Bill Strub dead."

"Yeah, cos' of your bullshit." Gleesty shook a finger at him.

"No time. In four minutes the charge of the mortar will change and kill stuff."

"Shit!" Gleesty snapped out of his negative thinking and lifted the heavy cannon, using it to plow through the door. With his other hand he covered his face with a gas mask. John followed right behind him.

That ye may eat the flesh of kings, and the flesh of captains, and the flesh of mighty men.

I jumped through the busted door and slammed into a male zombie. Dozens were behind him, all huddled together, continuing their speech. I did not bother turning the weed-whacker on to kill any; I just trotted down to my friends, knocking over anything undead in the way. They ignored us and just stared at the sky as they chanted.

I was shocked to pass through so many of them. Thousands in just a few feet. I tripped on intestines, skulls and feet. I felt saliva dripping down onto my head from zombies dangling out of windows.

I turned a corner and reached Main Street. John and Gleesty were a few feet away from me drenched in sweat.

"Two minutes, set it up before I lose count."

Gleesty turned the giant tube straight down the street. For some odd reason, John kicked the mortar so it was slightly crooked. Gleesty looked at John, confused, wondering why he would ever screw up his own plans.

And the flesh of horses, and of them that sit on them, and the flesh of all men.

"Okay!" John ran down the road in the opposite direction of where the strange rocket was pointing. "We need to get back 50 feet and somewhere safe!"

"What?!"

"Just climb this fucking ladder and don't die!"

We ran behind the slushgutter and headed for a large building. John jumped onto a fire escape and climbed up, we followed unsteadily.

John started singing, "3.14159265358979323846..."

"You fucking memorized Pi?!" Gleesty yelled.

"Before the alphabet!"

Both free and bond, both small and great.

We rushed to the rooftop of the building. The two zombies on top were quickly thrown off by Gleesty. The three of us huddled behind a ledge that was facing John's slushgutter.

"Thirty seconds...I think."

The lenses of our gas masks were all fogged up from the sweat that poured from our bodies. The gasps from my friends were almost as loud as the obnoxious apocalyptic singing.

"Couldn't have picked a better time, idiot," Gleesty muttered at John. "And you didn't even aim it properly! It's just going to hit a building!"

Fear Him, and give glory to him; for the hour of His judgment has come: and worship Him that defiled heaven, and earth, and the sea, and the fountains of waters.

The zombies stopped their chanting. They snapped out of their trance instantly and looked around, ready to hunt for flesh. They whipped their arms into the air and snarled.

John took off his mask and smiled, "These living sacks of flesh secrete so much oil and noxious fumes, I bet we can use them as ener-"

A loud *DUNKH* was heard; the charge of the mortar finally altered and the super magnet was released. The force of the mortar's recoil hit our building and shook it. The impact of the blast knocked back dozens of zombies and cars. A high-pitched wailing noise was heard as the rocket whirled down the street. A cone of rust, shrapnel, car doors, and pieces of buildings all spiraled up into the air and followed along down the road. Everything was being destroyed in an astounding rate. The amber fog turned bright red, coated with blood and continued to whip horizontally down the road. Cars were sliced in half, chunks of buildings were knocked off, and the manholes that were raked in cleared out the massive congregation of zombies. I looked at my friends who were peeking from the top of the ledge. John giggled maniacally. Gleesty removed his mask, showing us the tears in his eyes.

The noise was deafening. The magnet cleared out the fog and created a path for us. I removed my mask and witnessed the almighty power of the slushgutter. The streets and buildings were splashed with a tidal wave of blood.

"It's as if a hurricane was fucking a massive blender!" Gleesty shouted over the noise.

John raised his armed and yelled, "I love the smell of burnt flesh in th-"

The bullet hit a gas station. John's reason for turning the mortar at the last second was revealed. The electric charge from the inside of the bullet caused a massive explosion, firing out every single piece of metal that it collected on its journey and spraying fire down all over the town. It rained onto zombies that were streets away. The molten metal scraps caused hundreds of them to collect into a large conflagration; every walking dead that touched another was engulfed in flames. The streets lit up in a domino effect, pillars of fire rushed down street corners until its fuel ran out.

Gleesty stood up, ignoring the remains of the raining fire and ash. He clapped like a madman. "Done. Sold. Brilliant. Fuck. Fucking fuck." He grabbed John's hand and shook it. "That was a mighty annihilation. Yes, I am ready for death after that."

"Actually, that was supposed to kill us."

Gleesty paused, then, continued the hand shake with a brief chuckle. "Doesn't surprise me you sick bastard."

John looked down at the street. "Yeah, not too many zombies around the building. I say that I am completely satisfied with all the damage that I have caused and I am ready to die if the time comes soon."

"If you want to die, we can battle right now- take it like real men on a rooftop." Gleesty said.

"Nope, we're going to keep at it." John nodded his head. "I'm telling you, my uncle did not just waste his time on me."

"We're never going to save Mary's clone, or reach my parents." Gleesty said.

"We will." John scanned the side of the building where zombies began to walk down. "Look. My weapon pulled out a garage door. A truck!"

Gleesty looked down and spotted the truck, then turned to John. "I was just testing ya."

Eleventh Chapter

For the next upcoming streets, very few zombies littered the area. The ones that survived the blast ran viciously at us with a crown of fire consuming their shoulders. They collapsed a few feet in front of us when their brains burned any recognition of the virus. These zombies were definitely quicker than before. Their fierce grunting and lashing at the air disturbed me greatly. The thought of my friends charging at them with smiles behind their masks kept me going.

The moon was blood red in the late afternoon. The fog was absent in this section of the town; the red ash took its place. It trickled down from the sky and soothed my neck with its warmth.

"Mutt, we're going to split up," John grabbed the weed-whacker from my hands and shoved Gleesty towards his direction. "Grab what we left at the shop, we'll take the rest of this shit and pick you up." John threw the hammer tackers and a black backpack at Gleesty and ran off together before I could even react.

I acted on impulse and just ran for the gun shop. The hint of metal and burnt flesh was really getting to me. Even with the gas mask on, the nauseating fumes were giving me a migraine.

"Oh!" John halted halfway down the road. "Mutt! A piece of metal sliced part of your gas mask and almost killed you. Just. Uh." Then he whispered, "*Lettinyouknow.*"

"John!" I sighed.

"Tape it!" He disappeared behind the building with Gleesty.

The hole was directly under my nose, the perfect spot to royally distress me. I covered it with my hand and tried to endure my headache.

I could hear a hum from Gleesty blocks away, followed by the loud bursts of metal firing out of his gigantic staplers.

My hooves slammed against the pavement so hard that the mounds of ash under me exploded into a mushroom cloud. Every step I stomped harder, angrier, hurting the asphalt and cracking it beneath me. I wanted to open up hell itself with my galloping. I was angry and had no idea why.

And I looked up onto some buildings and saw the pessimistic nomads. Their silhouettes followed my movement. I tried to ignore their warble:

"The nations were angry, and your wrath has come. The time has come for judging the dead, and for rewarding your servants, the prophets, and your people who revere your name, both great and small...and for destroying those who destroy the earth."

I stopped in my tracks and turned to them. "How could this have happened?" I yelled.

"But for the fearful, and unbelieving, and abominable, and murderers, and fornicators, and sorcerers, and idolaters, and all liars, their part in the lake that burneth with fire and brimstone; which is the second death. " They all laughed as I shook my head.

The familiar beautiful female owl popped her head out of the crowd and smiled at me. "Isn't it eerie how a book from thousands of years ago could predict such a day as this?"

I took my gas mask off and looked at her with my red, watery eyes. "Was this Bill Strub's doing?" I yelled.

A few of them grunted. The female owl spoke up, "That old quack?" She waved her hands in front of her, brushing the ash away from her face. "I refuse to acknowledge such a misguided soul."

"But you all loved him! What happened? And John? What's wrong with John?"

They hissed like a struggling flame, their shadows turned away from me. "You are all to blame for this. So sit back and wait for your punishment."

There was no way I could reason with them to get some answers. How long have they been preparing for this to happen? I shook my head once more and turned away.

I ran into the old rendezvous point and searched for the supplies we left. Nothing. The place was ransacked. Everything was taken. I could only see the radio still on the same table and the katana sword resting behind the door. I looked on another counter and found an old torn up phone book. I peeled off a piece of scotch tape and sloppily applied it onto my mask. It dangled with poor craftsmanship, but it made me feel a little better.

What was I going to say to John? The Owls robbed us? No, they would never leave their stoops without good reason. The zombies took our belongings? I should have paid attention to our stuff. John is going to be angry. I cannot stand John angry.

The sound of the pickup truck roaring down the road caught my attention. I stepped outside, only to get hit with a rush of ash and a welcoming honk. Gleesty was standing in the cargo area of the pickup truck mask-less. The ash was all over him, his teeth were gray with dead burnt flesh.

"I'll take that!" Gleesty pointed to the sword. I handed it over. Gleesty tucked the long blade behind his ear like a flower. My feet carried me over to the passenger seat. John took his gas mask off and smiled. "Crazy weather we're having!"

"Not in the mood, asshole."

"Where are the supplies?"

"We were robbed by zombies."

"Weird..."

"All I found was that samurai sword there."

"Oh, I forgot to pick that up?"

"What?" I looked at John very confused.

"Oh, I took all of the stuff before we left. Three bottles of water, some canned bread, a handle of vodka, Bill Strub's book, flare gun, your gun, and you saw me with the other weapons."

"Oh," I looked down and made a sad face.

"Yep."

"So, why did you force me to run all the way back here and risk my life for nothing?"

"Well, Mutt, I wanted to use the weed-whacker."

I looked up at him. "You are quite possibly the worst human ever."

"Heeyyy. I needed mah killin' fix."

Gleesty pounded on the roof of the truck and yelled, "*Wah-wah-wah-waaahhhh.*"

"He knew too?"

"Yeah, I'm surprised he went through with the gag."

I sighed. The tape I fastened on the snout of my mask fell off. I sighed again.

John smirked. "I see you fixed your mask!"

"Please, let's just go." I turned and looked through the rear window of the truck, looking at Gleesty, sitting down at the rear of the cargo bin, adjusting his mask. "I feel bad for him, man."

"Hm?"

"So we get to sit here with the windows closed and he can't even fit in here. Why does it seem like his life is so difficult?"

"Oh shut the fuck up. He's the happiest, nicest person I have ever met." John rummaged underneath the seat and pulled out a little bag. "He got you a gift."

"What?" My eyes lit up in admiration. "Are you serious?"

"Yessir," John said, handing me the bag. I smiled and hugged it greedily.

I opened it up and looked inside. I turned to Gleesty with a bright red face. "YOU FUCKING ASSHOLE!"

"AHAHAHAHA!" Gleesty let out his legendary roar.

"Fucking horseshoes?!"

John laughed uncontrollably. "Oh yes that was brilliant. Are they your size?"

I opened up the window and chucked them out.

"Do you even know where you're going?

"Absolutely," John said.

"Gleesty told you the directions?"

"It's the Goresmith/CERN central. It's the biggest fucking building in the state. You need to get out more."

"I wouldn't be talking, buddy."

"Hmph," John grabbed Bill Strub's book that was resting on the edge of his seat. "Did you bother reading any of this?"

"Is that important right now?"

"Did you read any of this?"

"Well, yeah. I read the part on Spontaneous Human Combustion. Oh, he was right, by the way."

"Open to the last page."

"Why?"

"Don't tell me you're the only person that doesn't read the last page of a book first."

I shrugged and opened to the final page. It was stapled on.

John, me, or to whomever else opening this,

Now that this sacred tome has escaped my hands, I would like to tell my gentle reader that I am either dead, under arrest, or have evaporated. Now that I am gone, allow me to warn you of the unspeakable horrors that will happen. Actually, it probably has already occurred.

It was not a coincidence. Please head to my old headquarters. I have guided you with nothing but clues, in hopes that the Owls do not find me. Good thing I went ahead and made sure they lead to nothing but more clues.

Stay Bright, my child. So Bright.

P.S.
Bring Mutt.
-William Oz Strub

I slammed the book, accidentally shutting my fingers in the pages and laughed like an imbecile. John joined me in a laughing frenzy. Gleesty scratched his head.

"You had this planned all along?!"

"Just about. Some clues I have yet to unlock. The piece of shit lock box for example."

"Oh my god." My face was ready to burst with joy. "I feel just like I just watched a kitten fart."

"Excuse me?"

I shrugged.

"That was the very death note he left me."

"This is mind blowing. Does Gleesty know?"

"Actually, no. Not about Unc-"

We hit our first zombie. The vehicle remained still after its head was crushed under the wheel.

"The thinking plague," John said.

"Do you think God is punishing us?"

"Thought you were an Atheist..."

"Think I'm back at the Agnostic level."

"Fascinating."

"I have my reasons to believe." I closed my eyes and relaxed for a short while. Then I examined the windshield of the truck, slowly being chipped away by the rusted atmosphere. "Did I ever tell you of the man who shit larva?"

"Excuse me?"

"Well, once upon a time there was this fellow. He was an artist. He was an arrogant, cheap, piece of trash that was so used to getting everything he wanted when he was young that he expected it to continue on in his later years."

"So he was a brat?"

"Yeah, yeah. Well, he always complained about paying for rent, food, heat. The essential things that you need for living. He even complained about his water bill while he showered.

"Then one day, he saw something that he really wanted in a nearby store. It was this beautiful camera. It was so much money. He knew he couldn't afford it, and he scolded at everyone else, blaming his troubles on the innocent. A regular Scrooge.

"Another time, he cried out to God. He prayed for a straight hour, asking, begging for a better lifestyle. The next day he found these tiny red bumps on his skin. All over the place. They itched slightly, but nothing too significant. So after his mission at work, he went home and took a nap. He woke up with these tiny white larvae crawling out of his skin. From his back, ass, face, arms, it was all over the place. It didn't hurt, but it was just disgusting. He ran to the bathroom and looked at his face and vomited immediately. He fell back, crushing a great deal of these maggot-like creatures against the wall and passed out. When he came to, he tried everything he could to tear them all out. And they grew back. They grew back and died, and came back, and so forth. He would spend hours just having them crawl on his hand, then, crush them, like God, feeling powerful. He tried to kill himself many times, if he attempted with a razor blade, they would shield his skin and take the cuts, slowly dulling down the razor. If he tried anything spontaneous, these bugs would release a high-pitch squeal and take control over his actions.

"People found out, but they ignored him. He would cry and complain about shitting out worms and birds attacking him in the street for a quick meal."

"Keep going," John said, drooling all the while. "This is real tasty."

"He worked at home for his job. He submitted paintings, pictures, and drawings of himself covered in larvae. Everyone loved the art pieces, but they still knew that he deserved everything that happened to him.

"Then, he realized after a few weeks what was going on. These bugs cleaned him, they fed him by sacrificing themselves and crawling into his mouth. They kept him warm. His cost of living was low, and he gained money. And everything he ever wanted. These maggots were not an abomination, they were a blessing."

"I'd like to say I love this story, and you are telling me this because of these things here? These undead comrades of ours? Dare I say, people turning to religion?"

"Exactly."

"Yes, I see that very clearly."

"Do you think your uncle would enjoy being a zombie?"

"Oh, I think so. Personally, I feel that these things might truly be a way to achieve bliss."

I looked up at the roof of the truck. "How so?"

"When you die, chemicals are released into a euphoric orgasm. You experience this with that sex toy of yours. These people are technically dead, but only like, a near-death. No worries, pain, anxiety. Those chemicals might even be perpetual. All they want to do is eat for satisfaction. It's a literary numb for them."

"Numb," I nodded. "Perfect word. It's how I emotionally felt when Mary changed. It was only for a second. When she closed her eyes as a human, and opened them back up as an abomination, I just knew she wasn't there anymore. Numb is that feeling you get the second you throw all information of a loved one out and put a gun to their head."

"So, humans and zombies have something in common?"

We turned to the final block. Goresmith Facilities was down the street, faded in the fog. It emerged with welcoming friendly hands. It was only about thirty stories tall, but it could be 2 blocks in length.

John's magnetic firebomb could only kill so much. Zombies started to thicken up again.

The front of the Goresmith building had a great deal of landscape. Guards could be seen firing away at the dead with zero interest; they must have been at it for hours. After some fresh soil, there was a large iron gate that stopped the walking dead, followed by more landscape.

We hit another zombie. Its stomach ripped in two when she hit the bumper. John smiled when he saw them by the dozen, ready to intercept.

I turned around to look at Gleesty who held the katana in a bunting stance on the edge of the truck. He decapitated every single one that came near.

He rested the blade on the cargo bin and picked around for the flare gun and fired into the air.

Five-hundred feet away, the guards noticed our truck. They sounded a very calm alarm while shining a light that guided us to our destination. The gate slowly opened while guards continued their cleansing.

My heart stopped. Our destination was so close. The, amongst all of the zombies in front of us, I could see the dress of one that brought a memory of her smell. Mary. Mary was in front of us. Mary was about to die. I was no longer numb to her.

I acted on impulse. I grabbed the wheel and swerved the truck into a mound of debris. John yelled, confused, until I screamed Mary! He looked into my face and let go of the wheel.

We flipped three times and slid a few feet, just in front of the gate. I climbed out of the tipped over truck, John did the same.

"You okay?"

"Yeah, assface. Nice job. Where the fuck is Gleesty?"

Gleesty was fifteen feet away. One of his legs shattered through a curb, breaking his leg in the process. He yelled in pain. For the first time, I heard him yell in pain.

And the scariest moment of my life happened: A single zombie ran towards Gleesty, dug through his broken PVC pipe armor and bit him in the wrist. Gleesty looked at me with tears in his eyes, and a smile could be seen inside of his beard.

"No!" I charged for him, the katana blade stuck out of the ground. I grabbed it from the broken asphalt and advanced. "No! No! Glee!"

John's voice cracked. "Cut his fucking arm off!" He ran towards the soldiers, requesting aid.

Gleesty flung the zombies off of him. He raised his arms in the air, a plea for help. I panicked and ran to him. My adrenaline was off the charts. I could feel my heart pumping through my ears. I swung the blade down at his shoulder, cutting it off at the bicep.

Gleesty cried out to the guards. Once they realized that it was one of the boss's sons, they fought through the crowds in an incredible effort to save him.

John ran behind the officers, the expression on his face lead to me thinking that he was not all there. Gleesty was in shock, his eyes widened as he stared into mine. John laughed as blood fired out of Gleesty's shoulder.

I turned to John, ready to strike him next. "What the fuck is so fucking funny, John?!"

"Mutt," Gleesty turned to me with his mouth swung open. "You cut the wrong arm off, mate. Huh-Hah."

"Fuck!" I lifted the sword back up and cut the other one off, Gleesty bit his lip and cried.

"Oh my God. Oh my god." I repeated.

"Quick, cut his legs off too!" John yelled.

"He was bitten there?!"

"No, just so he can't kick the bucket!"

"That's not funny you sick fuck!"

Gleesty jumped up unsteadily and laughed. He was incredible. He could still walk *and* laugh even after losing so much blood.

"I could never get used to pain," he said. "But I could sure as fuck look forward to it." Gleesty ran for the gates and collapsed on a series of guards that lifted him up and carried him inside of the front doors of the building.

A soldier grabbed us both. "Get inside, now!"

We ran through the door, surprisingly, all the zombies disappeared for the time being. I did not see Mary, but she was the least of my concerns for now.

I writhed in anxiety. John's hands were shaking as we walked along the grass. He grasped the lock box like it was the only thing he had left. He realized what had happened, and the situation hit him hard. "John."

"Jackass," he replied.

"I-I know."

"He's fucked."

"Don't say that." I muttered when we entered the door.

"HE'S FUCKED!" His yell echoed in the large hallways. "HE'S GOING TO FUCKING DIE. Praise Valhalla, Mutt!" Tears rolled down his cheeks. "Once again Mary fucked you over. And at the cost of a great friend."

Twelfth Chapter

The sudden rush of adrenaline and anxiety died away and drowned in my sorrow. John and I sat on a bench near the entrance of the massive building. It felt like a living, breathing palace. The metal walls framing every door ventilated the freshest air I have ever tasted. We felt so lost in the hall. We were on the brim of the establishment, John looking at the well guarded entrance, probably retracing his memory and attempting to figure out how we could have fixed the past.

"Now what?" I said.

John snarled. "They told us to wait here." He looked back down to his feet. His voice grew heavy and dark. "Shut the fuck up and wait."

He really hurt me when he spoke. I took a deep breath and exhaled, admiring the pure air, trying to forget about my problems. There was a giant map of the entire building in front of us. I studied it; staring at the little star we were sitting on top of and followed the maze of rooms. It was split up in four main corridors in a big cross, much like the place I met Gleesty in. There was a military corner on the far right of the place, a medical clinic to the north, the biological facility to the south, and the residential area where we were settling in. This wing alone must have at least 900 residents alone, all resting in the hundreds of rooms scattered alongside of the place. This building was nothing more than a major laboratory before the epidemic. Now it's an all-purpose safe house.

I turned my attention to the other side of the hall. The crowds of people in the chambers and in the halls did nothing but complain for food and drugs. The sorrow in my heart grew dense. None of these humans were like Gleesty. I will never find a person as humble and warmhearted as my friend.

"How did it feel?" John asked.

I was taken aback by this question. "I feel wrong."

"Yeah. So now what?"

Guilt and hesitation stalled me for about ten seconds before I answered the question. "John, you can go ahead and stay here until this blows over. I have to keep my promise, even if it means we have to part ways."

John nodded. Then stomped his foot, cursing. "Look at these folks. That's one good reason I should have made mends with the Owls."

A little girl skipped by in front of us and glared at my eyes like they were crystal balls. Her curiosity and innocence calmed me. I waited for her to say something, but all she did was smile and walk back down the hallway.

The grunts and cries grew louder as a man in a white robe walked in our direction. The static in the room lead me to standing up and staring at the man. John got up as well. He stopped right in front of us, and after he took his last step, the noise died down drastically. He was tall, bulky and handsome, probably of Irish and Russian descent. Then, the stench of wet leather hit me.

"My name is Doctor Odradek Goresmith," he hid his face behind the clipboard. When he extended his hand for a shake, I took a peak at the paper clipped down and saw that it was blank.

I extended my dirty hand to shake his. He hesitated at it, but grabbed it anyway. "Please, we really need answers sir. What is going on with our situation? Will other countries start bombing us? Gleesty? Are the Owls right? Sir?"

Odradek sighed. "Gleesty...uhm...Gleesty..."

"I want to see my fucking uncle," John barked.

Odradek was not surprised with John's attitude. He nodded and cleared his throat. "My friends, there is plenty of time to explain everything. Now Mutt..."

I loved the way he said my name. He was so warm and kind. His patience made me admire him. Normally, I hated doctors, but it felt like he knew me for years. And his calm tone gave me hope that Gleesty was still alive and well.

"Mutt, I really must know right now," he said. "Were you ever bitten?"

I looked at him, then, glanced at John. "No."

"Thank God," he rubbed his eyes and nodded. "I supposed I will start with this. Follow me."

We walked on, following this man in the long halls and turns throughout the place while he spoke. I think the calmness of him loosened up John. His breathing returned to normal. I looked down at John's right hand and smiled at the fingers poking in the keyhole of the lock box. Various trashcans were scattered throughout the area, so we began picking off some of our clothing. My gas mask was gone, probably still outside. John and I tore off our PVC pipe armor. I looked at his back pocket and saw one of the hammer tackers that he made for Gleesty. My stomach stopped aching in pain once I removed the chest piece. When I looked down at my body, I noticed how dirty I was. Disgusting. My gun was blatantly peering out of its holster. Nobody seemed to care, so I walked on with it.

"I suppose "zombies" is the popular term for them. Now, these zombies are quite something. They continue to spread, mutate, and dare I say evolve." He said this while he rubbed his nose and nodded at every worker that walked by.

"They were slow at first because of the rigor mortis. They were practically handicapped and were very weak for the first few hours. And even then we couldn't control them. Superiority in numbers, I suppose."

"Right," John interrupted. "And now they move without a problem."

"Right," the doctor muttered. "They are stronger."

"The virus works in a unique way. As you can probably already tell, it strictly moves toward the brain first, seizing the medulla and planting itself into the hypothalamus. From there, it spreads and makes a vacant lot in the mouth. The victim is now a host, but it reverts back to a primal state where we humans only required basic needs to survive. Shelter and food. This odd parasite, as we witnessed not too long ago, is controlled by, well, a higher source. Its agenda is to eliminate all of us by turning us against each other. To fight fire with fire, you could say. However, the virus requires an incredible amount of energy to thrive. We thought that if we controlled the area, they would starve themselves. We were very wrong. While the mind craves flesh, the body hardly requires it. It can absorb the necessary food right outside. The rust fuels them. They remind me of the carnivorous pitcher plant after examining several autopsies. They are, how do I say it, acoelous."

I looked at myself again. Steel-rot engulfed my clothes and fur. The dry blood slowly chipped away from my hooves. The ashes hid beneath my little hairs and tingled behind my ears.

"Yes," I said. "We heard much about it on the radio."

He nodded. "Now, the virus has some interesting features. It does not want the body to die in the least. It has the ability to break down certain substances on our earth to create antagonists and mimic certain drugs, such as adrenaline. They are in a constant rage and are now much harder to fight. The head now needs to be completely destroyed before a single one dies. It's like hunting a lion."

"So that means we are fucked?" John asked.

"I'll get to the fucking later." Odradek said. "Mutt, I hate to break it to you but you are a mutant."

"I...I know."

"Okay, good." He laughed at himself. "Now, I am sure you are aware that there are several of your types out there. Some not as lucky as you."

We reached a large sign that read *Military Quarter*. We walked past several other doctors and soldiers and through large barred doors. I glanced around as we continued along through the hallway that was tinted with green lights. As we past large cubicles, I witnessed odd vehicles and weapons being tested. We took a left, then a right, inside of a massive room that had nothing in it. I examined each corner, and even suspected that it was a trap. I positioned my cracked hooves next to the doctor; in case anything funny happened I could at least get a nice shot at Odradek's knees.

Odradek flipped a switch. The wall in front of us slowly opened up, revealing a gigantic glass wall caked with frost. On the other side was nothing but darkness. Odradek flipped another switch that triggered a heater. The frost slowly began to dissolve. A final switch; and the lights on the other side were turned on. We moved in closer, now standing five feet away from the window. I saw 8 inch thick bars after the glass, then, a familiar face.

Odradek's voice was mighty, empowering and soothing. When he spoke, it made me feel like I could conquer anything. "He killed an incredible amount of people. There are plenty more of them out there, also infected." John's gasp was slowly overtaken by a giggle.

In front of us was a gigantic zombie boar wrapped in chains; the blood and mashed bones protruding from his body was enough to give me another heart attack. Surrounding the creature was a machine, just as high as the boar sat-approximately 11 feet. My God, sitting down, it was 11 feet high. The machine was emitting cold air that had a strange sleep effect on the mutant. The piercings now dwarfed his nose and the frozen snot was encrusted around the jewelry. I couldn't believe it was him.

He used to be just six feet tall. I told Odradek that his size probably tripled and he just nodded with an unsurprised look on his face.

"These beasts are followed around by a horde of *them*."

"What George Orwell would give to see something like this," John licked his lips. His eyes wanted him to break through the glass, bend the bars and conquer the beast, riding him throughout the nation with a trident in his hand shrieking 'majesty!'"

"Cold air slowed this one down. We had to throw sixteen nets the size of Olympic pools at him with helicopters to stop him. He isn't even the biggest one."

"What are you going to do with him?"

"What kind of fucking petting zoo will take this piece of work? We've been thinking about killing it, just ending it right now. Of course, many scientists are dying to learn more about it. But this, this is too much. The only thing that's keeping us from getting killed by this monster is that massive air conditioner. The pure air inside has weakened it significantly."

John looked at all of us with a smile, "maybe we should let it go, this is cruel." He then leaned backwards, cracked his back and shook his head violently. John straightened up and looked at me in admiration. "You would look *so* marvelous as a zombie."

Odradek interrupted with a cough. "We have also been thinking about tapping into its brain, maybe controlling the beast ourselves, but it's so damn risky. Now, I have learned much about the both of you, but from what I've been told in such a short period of time, I am going to have to postpone our business for later tonight at dinner."

"And will Gleesty be there? It's my-"

"Gleesty is *my* patient. But right now, I cannot tell you the status of his condition."

John then cracked his neck. "You have to do better than that, doc."

Odradek wasn't offended by this at all. He looked like he was up all night. I couldn't see it before, but he was absolutely exhausted. The dark bags around his eyes reminded me of rotting slugs. "He is alive. His mission was successful at least."

"Mission?"

"That- I will explain later. It may seem we have used him, but we love him very much. Now please, you will be escorted to your room; shower and rest. You've come a long way in such a catastrophe."

John and I were confused at why he was so upfront about "using him", but we shook his hand and parted ways. Odradek's way of talking now put us in suspicion. A guard escorted us to the front door of our living space. Everyone was quiet. The phosphorescent lights were the only thing I concentrated on to drown out the moaning and crying from our fellow residents. The guard who remained silent the entire time nodded his head, informed us the door was opened, and said good-bye.

"They've got a lot of explaining to do," John said.

"No shit. I'm ready to piss my pants from the suspense." My body wanted rest, but my brain needed more. The adventure gave me an apocalyptic high. Drugs suddenly lost their appeal."

"Maybe you need your fix, Mutt."

"Maybe, but you know what, I'm going to kick it."

"Leaving your precious drugs?"

I nodded. "Yeah, like Odradek said. We're lucky ones, aren't we?"

John nodded. He looked relieved with my decision, but could probably care less. I should stay clean, that way I could get a good first impression in on Mary's clone.

I had to know if the clone was still alive- if the building was even still standing. Would it be worth asking to be transported there, or should me and John sit and wait for everything to blow over and care for Gleesty? I couldn't imagine him leading a normal life without any arms. I have heard of technology being good enough to clone limbs and reattach them to the person, but that could take months.

I already missed him. He really was an incredible friend. I have never been in a dispute with him, unlike John, who attempts to prove me wrong in any given situation. Gleesty nodded at everything I said, gave input into my decisions. He proved that he would die for me and die without regretting it. His heart is rich with compassion. His father seemed to be just as caring, perhaps a little stubborn or maybe arrogant with his success, but I couldn't blame him. Odradek was intelligent, attractive, rich and powerful. He tore down a quarter of his main building to aid the people. And what am I doing now with my life? Pursuing a clone that belonged to a whore? She's dead and I'm still wrapped around her finger.

I looked at John with glossy eyes and thought about his uncle. If he is here, we are in good hands. If we cannot figure out the mysteries of this day, we at least can be reunited again.

More thoughts circled me. I was overwhelmed now after having no time to think; just moments away from an anxiety attack, ready to fall to my knees and vomit all over John's shoe.

John raised an eyebrow. "What's on your mind?"

I sighed. "Nothing. just want to shower."

I walked into the bathroom and saw a few towels, toothbrushes and soap for us. Sweatpants and some plain white cloth t-shirts were placed inside the drawers below the sink. The thought of me being clean again excited me too much. I tore off the rest of my clothes and leaped into the shower.

The water hitting my body was slowly picking off my problems. My mind was at ease as all of the mud, blood, metal and sweat flowed down my body and seeped into the drain. Small rust flakes flew out of my mane and splattered onto the ceramic walls. I examined their dark glittery little faces. I let some water into my mouth and fired at the little shavings that resembled lost ants. The black ooze that was pouring out of my mouth scared the shit out of me. It rained down and joined the rest of the grime. I shrugged and continued to clean myself.

After cleaning myself off I put my clothes on, darted out of the room and leaped on top of the bed. My hoof hit the bedpost and put a crack in the oak wood carving. I shrugged and rubbed my face into the pillow while I hummed a cheerful melody. John looked at me with surprise at how clean and bright my face was. He arose from the bed and walked into the bathroom with curiosity. I looked at the clock- 6:30 pm. I crammed my head inside of the two pillows and closed my eyes. But I could not sleep yet, my fidgeting and twisting went on for minutes until I opened my eyes back up and looked at John's bed. Bill Strub's book, the one that joined us in our mission, was resting there on the pillow. My limbs pulled me to it and my body followed. Something compelled me to open it. I began reading the first few pages.

September 9th - It is True Infinity in which I seek. God is infinite. Therefore, God is the ultimate equation. If I can form the perfect continuum theory, much like Cantor's or Godel's work, I can find a map to God. Boltzmann shall guide me, but he will not limit me.

December 13th – So it begins. All logic is flawed. However, probability is unfazed by this. Since probability suffers from uncertainty, it can pass through the cracks of flawed logic. This is where I foresaw the future. My work has lead me to the Twenty-Year Glimpse. I must alert the superiors of the Super Entropy. My years of being called the Count of Counter-Intuitive shall be remembered no more.

It was all so interesting, but almost impossible to understand, if not idiotic. I turned the page to a list of inventions he created. I've not heard of a single one. Probing machines, vehicles that drifted over oil, the reinvention of the ornithopter- which primarily ran on magnets and liquid nitrogen. He even invented odd metals and gems.

Even though he made less and less sense the older he grew, it did not seem like most of these theories were just interpretations. Bill must have gone out of his way to perform and create his mad ideas. He has proof; the pictures pasted in the tome were enough for me. Perhaps when he was younger he was not as crazy, back when he used to work for the Goresmiths. John and I were about to find out something extraordinary. I could feel it.

I closed the book and went to my bed for rest.

No dreams, just a dry, clean, sleep. A hand grabbed my tail and tugged on it until I woke up. I let out a high nay.

"Come on," John said. "It's eight. Dinner time."

I opened my eyes and saw John with a very fancy suit on. I looked at my clothes and sighed. "Whose funeral did you just get out of?"

"My own, now let's go."

"No, really, where is my suit?"

"Probably in the barn next to the salt lick. Let's go!"

I grunted. "John, we have to chat."

He sighed and sat on my bed, resting his elbow on one of my legs. "Okay, what?"

"We have no idea what to expect from them. Gleesty never spoke about his parents, he didn't seem to like them. We'll probably hate them. He was, you know, teased about his size. He was called a Neanderthal, a barbarian, a savage viking. And look at me. Hell, look at *you*! They know your insane uncle, and here you are dressed like you just left a very exclusive rape party, are ya with me? They will treat us like expendable trash."

John nodded. "Yeah, I'm the Mother Theresa of sodomy. Listen, just bite the bullet and go. They invited us to a dinner, they must think highly of us. And they don't know what to expect from us either. Maybe the ball isn't in their hands, maybe they need *us*."

"I'm afraid of the truth." My hooves were now clacking against the bedpost in an abstract rhythm.

"Then stay here."

"Hell no. I owe Glee that much." I thought about him for a few seconds. Then Mary. Oh, God, Mary. The primary allure. "Okay let's go."

We opened the door and walked in silence. The muddy footprints of nearby residents guided us around the corner to a guard that sent us to an exclusive area. The cries of the residents have yet to die down. Guns shots could be heard outside.

We headed for the silent halls. In front of us stood a giant wooden door, probably the only door in the entire building that was wooden. It opened.

The first thing we saw was a 14-foot wooden table smothered with food and overwhelmingly large ornaments. A roast pig with the classic red apple rested on the left side of the table. A real apple. In the center lay dozens of exotic sea animals. Foods from all countries and cultures. There were seven bottles of wine; one in each corner and three in the middle in front of several candles. Finally, on the other end of the table was something I have never seen before. Something so beautiful it instantly raised my spirit to a point where I could smile at John; A gigantic ice sculpture of a massive tree. Every branch was a splintered arm grasping an exotic fruit. Several hands on a single branch and only two types I could identify on Yggdrasil, dragon fruit and star fruit. The only thing missing in this room was a fried balding eagle.

Two men sitting on the opposite side of the table from where we're standing suddenly smiled at us. They stood up, heads nodding, and extended their hands for a shake, we followed through with it. They were still in their work clothes, both with white jackets like the other scientists. Both very attractive men, tall, thin, with dark reddish hair. I swear one could be a clone of the other.

Near the ice tree sat a female, a very attractive mother. And to the left of the table was Odradek, already standing waiting for one of us to say something. The Goresmiths looked completely different from Gleesty. And I scanned the room for the portraits of their ancestors, all with a flag behind their bodies. France, Italy, Greece, America, England, South Africa, and many others. Not in any particular chronological order, you could tell how long ago the paintings were dated back just by how weathered they were. And none of the females and males looked anything like my old friend. Except one-the portrait just above John. A painting of a man named Grigori Rasputin.

We had no idea what to say, what to do. The room was full of so much information that we wanted.

Odradek sat down. "Please, boys, just sit. We have much ground to cover."

We both took our seats.

"Our family tradition is to eat first. Indulge a mighty feast. Save the big stuff for later. There's much to swallow."

The food was like nothing I've ever had before. My parents had me survive on canned food and boxes of crackers. Bill Strub fed me close to nothing because he believed in fixed starvation. But this feast was one that I wished would never end. We started at the pig and worked our way across the table, devouring everything that they stacked on our plates. Servants ran back and forth from the other doors and cleaned up.

"Mutt," John said with a grin. "If you eat a donkey, is that cannib-"

"Shut the fuck up John nobody cares," I muttered.

At one point of the feast one of the brothers, Set, brought up the idea of a theory called "dark flow" that involved the universe. John looked at him in disgust as he rattled the fork in his hand. Set was not moved by John's attitude in the least, and even smiled at him. His perfect white teeth looked almost faux, as well as his body in general. I just could not get over how fake they appeared to be.

"Well?" John said with a crooked smile.

"I'm so sorry that our son couldn't be here. But let me formally introduce my other two. As you know Set's name, he is the head of the military and technology quarter of my foundation. Now my other, Purr; he is ahead of my human resources, medical and agriculture studies. Mutt, you may have seen him before."

I took a good look at Purr. The silent man opened up his soul to me with his dark eyes. He looked just like any other rich doctor. I shook my head.

"The care center."

"Ah."

John slammed his lock box and the table. I pressed my fingers to my forehead. "John, please."

"Listen, I'm sick and tired of this world. In my life I have probably inhaled about 52 dollars in change from this fucking atmosphere. My uncle left me to care for a mutant that w-"

"Please! Sir!" Odradek's wife stood up. Maritza Goresmith. She had a strong heart, her eyes widened with joy every time John and I spoke. "Please. It's been tough on all of us."

John sighed and shook his anger off. "Should I be worried about Gleesty?"

"Heaven's no," she said. "My son will be just fine. I just do not want any tension between us. We are so happy that both of you are alive."

"But we maimed your son!" John's voice choked. "I've never met any of you before, and the closest member of your family has been struck down by us." John looked at them all. The perfect, rich, gorgeous family. I knew exactly what he was thinking. Gleesty did not belong in this portrait. "He looks so strange compared to all of you, I'm sorry, but he does. Was he adopted?"

Odradek chuckled.

Purr opened his mouth. "Gleesty is unique, yes. He stands out from this family of ours. I'm sure he has told you nothing but negative things about us, if he even did mention us. He can say whatever he wants about my brother and me. He is the person that I respect the most, and my little brother fought hard in his mission to bring you here."

"What is it about this mission?" I muttered. There was an uncomfortable pause, followed by reassuring smile from the family. "I'm glad you are all smiles, and I appreciate your concern for your family member, but these doom-mongers and the walking dead are really doing a number on my mental health. We have a lady friend of ours to save and if I don't get any feedback right now I think I am going to go batshit insane." I felt my blood pumping. The pressure echoed into my ears. It was worst anxiety attack I will ever experience. "Nobody cries thinking about their own funeral, dad?" Tears fell on the tablecloth. I muttered more nonsense until John calmed me down by petting my mane. The smiles dropped, I heard a few apologies and pulled myself together.

"We have several ways to deal with the plague. I mean to get rid of it, that is."

"And my friend's clone? Can we get her first?" I just wanted to find this poor girl. "She's at a cloning facility."

"Gleesty has mentioned it to us a few times." Odradek looked promising. I just couldn't take Odradek seriously anymore. His facial expressions and tone of voice never changed. Our nation is full of so much regurgitated pride. All plans and solutions were nothing more than repeated answers that our ancestors from generations ago attempted. Nothing was new or daring. Nobody cared for the expendable ones.

"Your friend in the cloning facility may be a bit more difficult for us. Do you know the lab she is at?"

"Newark." I said.

"Okay." Set said. "My yard. That lab is intact. The clones, however-some have been shipped out. Do you know her name?"

My jaw dropped. "I know her, uh, mother's name, it's Mary."

"Last name?"

John slammed his head on the table trying to remember. I just shook my head.

"That's not good." Purr said.

"Wait, wait." Set shook his finger at his brother. "I have an idea, it may be risky though."

Odradek stood up. "Set, they are staying here."

"No." Tears were filling my eyes. "I have to find her. Even if I have to go alone."

"Very well," Odradek sat back down. He probably felt like he just made an ass of himself. "I won't argue."

"I can't bring every single clone here. Too many, not enough time, and I can't remove them from their stations just yet. I can, however, send you over with our next supply truck."

"No helicopter?"

He sighed. "I really cannot. I'm sorry. They are all on a strict patrolling agenda. I can have one follow you, though. Please, don't worry. The truck will be armed with soldiers and turrets. I mean, the truck itself is nearly impossible to break into. Now, you can go and try to identify her, if she's an exact replica that is. We'll just line up all the soldiers as well when you get there. I know it's a weak plan."

Odradek's wife spoke up. "Can't we just send out a photograph of Mutt? Maybe she can identify him?"

"She's never met me before. And I know so little of her parent."

"And she's your friend?" Set blurted out.

"Is that your business?" John asked.

I interrupted. "This all sounds fine to me. Our original plan was like this anyway."

Odradek nodded. "We will arrange the transportation very soon." He pulled out a special type of cell phone and started typing up a message. "We will keep you notified. Now, before we cut to the serious stuff, I want to tell you all something that just happened."

"Glee-"

"No, no, nothing about Gleesty. It's about the zombies. Many of them have grown very aggressive. They all follow ringleaders, most of them mutants like Mutt here.

You all probably know this. But before I begin to describe how the STD came to be, I have to tell you that the victims are, well, um. They are laughing."

"Laughing zombies?" Set asked. "You didn't mention this earlier, pa."

"Not really a bad thing." John said. "Lighten up the mood, yanno?"

Silence.

"So," I said. "Zombies are laughing."

"They have plenty of reasons to," John blurted out.

Odradek interrupted with a chuckle. "This disease we're dealing with has the incredible ability to, well, *accept* other viruses. It pretty much fuses itself with anything harmful against us. Now, you are all probably skeptical about this being controlled by a higher power, but let me tell you this right now. Our nation has a crucible of different people from different lands. Well, someone from Papua New Guinea must have been around here, because our little dilemma just got worse."

"Kuru?!" John smiled.

Odradek nodded.

"What's a Kuru?" I asked.

"It is one of the rarest diseases known to mankind. You can only get it from consuming a human brain. The disease is also called the Mad Human Disease. Or the laughing sickness."

"Oh, Jesus Christ," I sighed and accidentally blew a candle out. "We have an audience laughing at us."

"Indeed," Odradek nodded. "We've nicknamed them Gigglers. There are a handful of them now, but I'm sure there will be plenty to deal with. Oh, another thing!"

"You are just full of great news, old man." John said.

"While I do not agree with it, the media feels that we cannot call them zombies anymore. It's not politically correct and very offensive."

"That's ridiculous. What do we call them?"

"COPs."

"Excuse me?" John and me were both astounded and enraged with this new name.

"Casualties of Perdition."

Purr laughed. "That was a joke. Ignore my father."

We shook our heads in disgust and decided to move forward in the conversation. "Will these, that is, the Gigglers, affect my plans?" I said.

"Most likely not. It'll just be a bit more annoying. The truck you are taking is fifteen-feet tall, divided into two 40-foot sections, and moves with trails. It runs over just about anything." Odradek pulled out a photograph of it from his pocket and showed it to John and me. It was exactly what he described, but I still felt uneasy.

"I see that it's divided in the middle for a turn radius, but it seems like that is a weak spot for it." John said as he pointed to the center of it. It was true. The middle was a long divider mostly connected with rubber.

"Yeah, which is why we have two people steering the vehicle. The first half of our truck is supplied with food, medicine and weapons. The latter half is where we will be transporting you, as well as a various set of soldiers. We have to ship some clones back to cleanse their blood and support the lab in Newark."

"And these troops will be armed?" I asked.

"Yes, they most certainly will be. We've equipped every single worker with the finest assault rifles. Oh, and Mutt, we've all seen that old pasty M9 attached to your chest there. Why not trade that in and get a nice rifle? Perhaps maybe a Carcano?" He let out a slight chuckle. I watched his nose hairs dangle and dance like a baby millipede.

"No, thank you. It won't be necessary." I placed my palms on the table and leaned back in my chair.

"But- it's so outdated."

"Yes, but it belonged to my father, before he shot himself in the head." Everyone in the room glared at me in shock.

"I'm, uh." Odradek's gentle voice made me realize how much of a jerk statement that was. "I'm sorry, Mutt."

I shook my head and apologized. "Sorry, that was rude."

"Well, please let me set you up with a gun anyway, just in case?"

"Me too?" John blurted out.

The rich family laughed. "No, you're off your rocker. We've known that for months," Maritza said.

Odradek's eyes widened.

Then, John lingered on a pause. He stared at the doctor, then at Purr and finally at Set. "How?" He leeched information from the silence. My friend lowered his head, slammed his eyes shut and kicked at a table leg. "Oh my God."

"What?" I was so confused with John's behavior- everyone's behavior, actually. "What?"

"Mission," John rattled.

"Uhm," Odradek reached into his pocket and pulled out his glasses. John placed the lock-box on the table and pointed a corner of it towards Odradek. "Several months ago, Mutt, you were in one of our rehabilitation centers. You were heavily monitored because of your condition, which lead us to some very important information, what your existence may portend. More importantly, you lead us to finding a friend of ours who ran away and just disappeared. William Oz Strub. We did sort of kidnap him, but we most certainly gave him a day's notice."

"Fuck, fuck, fuck, fuck, fuck, fuck!"

Fuck, fuck fuck fuck. My heart was racing. I was expecting a butter knife to enter my skull by John's hands at any moment.

"When we first worked with him, he was working under a different alias-Herbert Mason, sometime before John was born. When you gave those manuscripts of his to our son Gleesty, we immediately knew it was work done by our old companion. We sent Gleesty to watch after you while we watched our Dr. Strub."

This family set us up the entire time. Gleesty was there just to guard us from danger. It started to make sense now. It was Gleesty who always pulled through in the end when John and I got into fights with hoodlums. He was the one who always paid for our drinks. It was his idea to go here first. I looked at John, whose face was red. I looked at him with my big almond eyes while my sagging mane brushed at my forehead. We should not be mad at Gleesty. I did cut his arms off after all. I can understand why John was so angry. Bill and Gleesty have secrets, and this strange brainwashed child resents secrets.

"Odradek," I said. "What kind of projects did Bill do for you?"

"Listen, Bill, or however you may call him, was revered amongst the Owls for what he had done."

"Wait, how did the Owls find out?" I asked.

"There were others who worked here that engaged in mutiny. They all had separate reasons why, but most of them simply had a major grudge against us. Gentlemen, Oz Strub is the reason why we have so much pollution in our atmosphere."

John looked at me and then back at Odradek. "For some reason, now don't call me crazy, but I am not surprised."

"Heh," Odradek reached into his front coat pocket and placed an odd grayish block on the table.

"Goresmith spread the tale that the origins of the debris were started by your high industry and energy consumption rate." I said. "You managed to profit off of it, and here we are. It's pretty harmful, I mean, plants and animals don't seem to mind, but it is quite a nuisance to my sinus. And it somehow keeps the zombies going? So, explain."

"Do you know what this is?" He slid the metal block to us. We shook our heads. "We nicknamed it Negativium. John, it was invented about 20 years ago by that mentor of yours. The most pointless metal of all time. It is just a useless piece of shit. It is softer than lead, is a very poor conductor, and has no magnetic value."

Odradek set up a smile on his face while he dug into another pocket and pulled out a gadget. It looked like a very fancy laser pointer. He shined the red light onto the metal and it rapidly began to deteriorate. "That's why I wanted to eat first," he laughed as the little shavings of metallic dust floated into the air. "It, however, absorbs radiation, a great deal of it." He pointed the laser onto the table and it instantly ate away at the wood. "And when it does, well, that happens. All that rust. But now it has magnetic traits, and is a decent conductor. He was so proud of this invention. We didn't know why, while it was much better than other UV shields, it still breaks down and makes a mess."

John scratched his head. "Alright, so he tried to kill us all by firing a laser into this brick to poison us? It doesn't surprise me in the least."

"No. Twenty years ago, this planet was supposed to be destroyed." The doctor sighed and looked at the hole that the laser created. "Bill was lucky enough to discover something before it hit us off guard."

"He saved us?" John asked.

"He did. A stray star hit us with a major solar wind. Bill constructed a metal that countered the effects."

"We nicknamed it the Morning Star," Set said. "Bill claimed that he saw it in his dreams. He said it was a vision from God. God told him that he was upset at humans and wanted to test them again."

"That's completely ridiculous," I said. "Why Bill?"

"Who knows," Set said. "But lo and behold, he came to us with a discovery by pinpointing a location in the universe with the Fibonacci numbers. This was when he was a scientist here, after his military service."

"Enough, boys," Odradek said. "Both of you were just kids." Odradek coughed up some rust and lifted a magnet into the air, sucking up all the hovering fragments. "We thanked Bill and his team for their work and saving the Earth. But he became paranoid and arrogant. The solar wind came six months after his discovery. We, of course, mass produced the metal to save us all. In those six months, Bill went back and forth, canceling the operation, resuming the production, killing innocent people in his terrible experiments. First he said we deserve to be destroyed, then, the following week he would apologize and continue his work.

"Three months before the coming catastrophe, he told us that in 20 years, we would see a part two of the ordeal. He never went in full detail with this one. We waited for another solar wind to bathe our faces in. We weren't expecting *this*.

"For 20 years, our heads were raised at the sky. We never bothered to look down."

"What else did Bill do?" John asked.

"When the solar wind hit, he claimed himself as a Messiah. He said God hadn't spoken to him in months, so he demanded that we sacrifice our brains to him. It was too much. When the fog came, the media clamored. We blamed it on your uncle and his followers. Most of them are now those hermits on the rooftops of abandoned buildings. We purposely leaked information that the people, now Owls, were corporate leaders that royally screwed up.

"Before Bill fled the state, he took his dead step-brother's name and disappeared for several years. I'm sure you and John can fill the spaces there. Then, 6 months ago, well, you know the rest."

"Okay," John said. "Let's take a step back for one fucking minute. Are you still producing Negativium?"

Odradek nodded.

"Why? Can't you just stop producing it? It's fueling the zombies anyway, correct? If it slowly dwindles, maybe they will die off, or at least cripple them in way."

"We've thought of it. We can even wipe out the rest of the miasma easily with an operation closely related to nuclear fission. "Odradek coughed again and cleared his throat. "But it ruins our initial plan. See, there is still too much radiation in the air. If we don't at least have the metal to muddle it, we will slowly fry."

"So we die from radiation or we turn into zombies?"

"Pretty much. Thing is, we've studied this phenomenon for two decades. It would only be 5 more years before the radiation would diminish and we would be able to breathe fine air outside once more. But then this happened under our noses." Set said this like the smug smart-ass child that he was.

"All of you have been hiding this from the public for two decades?" I raised my voice. "You're one of the most trusted organizations out there that has actually benefited from all of this. It makes me sick. You control the country, managed to break passed a monopoly loop and put so many damn lives in danger." They all leaned back in their chairs, waiting for me to explode. "And yet, you can't even fucking provide me with a fucking helicopter to find a friend of mine?! Are you all fucked in the head? Gleesty was right. He was absolutely right. You're all just smug assholes that lack courage. Fucking scoundrels. You aren't even close to his greatness, and I don't even care if he was in on it from the beginning. He at least stuck his neck out for us with his own muscle. We weren't even important! None of you are even close to what he was built to become."

And they all nodded. I looked at the mother, who passed a photograph face-down across the table. "You are right, dear. This was Gleesty when he was a few years old. This is what he used to be."

I turned the picture over, looked at it, and showed John. I couldn't believe it at first, until I looked into the child's eyes. They were gray and powerful. But the body and face was nothing similar to his figure now. He stood like a twig, his wrists and legs thinner than my tongue. I've never seen someone so disfigured in my entire life.

"What is this?" I asked.

"Our family, as you can see from the portraits, comes from a long blue bloodline. Our rich ancestors partnered themselves with incredible historic figures. Genetic breeding and the right teachers have brought us up as top-tier humans. But our other son does not have much luck in his life."

John stared at the photograph for a long time without blinking. "And our friend was the genetic flusher?"

"Well," Purr shrugged. "Yes. Gleesty is the runt."

I looked at the photograph some more. I rubbed my hand across my mohawk and shook my head violently. "You experimented on him."

Set nodded. "Gleesty was inferior. We only wanted to give him a decent life, and please, hold your fire. He asked for it. He even begged and promised he would dedicate his life to helping others if his wish came true. So we experimented on him. Rapid hormone growth, dozens of bone structure surgeries, steroids, testosterone, it was all done to him and it was an incredible success. He was so grateful. And if you look up there, he admired our two Russian ancestors that resembled him, a Viking by the name of Ivan the Red. And the hardest man to kill, Grigori Rasputin."

"I admire the family tree, no matter how unnatural it may seem," John said. "But I want to know, where is our friend now?"

"Father's been working hard. We just hope that he doesn't become one of them."

"How long until we know he is fine?" I asked.

Odradek glanced at his cell phone and looked back at us. "We're not sure yet, but we do know both of you will be shipped off in two days."

"Jesus," I sighed. "So tell me, if this thing ever blows over, what the hell are you going to do? I think you owe the world much. I'm sorry that you are taking this from a little person like me, but I've lived in this mess with *him* and have never seen a blue sky. You've all at least had the pleasure of that."

Odradek nodded. He did not seem to mind my behavior. "We will shut ourselves down and give away our entire production to smaller branches and accept a lower part in the system. We hate what we have become. So drunken with power. We've been trying to protect the inevitable for far too long. Maybe we should have never stepped in, but right now, we have Bill."

John rubbed his eyebrow in uncertainty. "I am simply amazed that you would say that. Especially to us, what favors did we ever do for you?"

"We made a promise to Bill to protect you if he came with us."

John shrugged. "He hardly cares about us."

"That's not true," Odradek said.

"Come on," John said. "Do you think he's in that lab making something good? He's probably going to kill us all. Bill grew sick and tired of waiting to watch us all fail. I don't know his theories on everything, but I do know that he started losing it when my father died."

"Your father?" I said.

"Yes. They were both drafted in a war that took place 25 years ago. They were drafted while in college. Under the stars one night, when you could still see stars clearly, they had a chat about math. Bill said that's what calmed my father during the gunfire- like the sound of a waterfall. Then, an explosion was heard. When they stood up from the little trench they made, they were gunned down. My dad was killed, Bill survived a gunshot to the head. I think that bullet messed Bill up a little bit, actually."

"John," I said. "How do you expect me to believe that? It was 25 years ago. You're 20. There's a gap there."

"Might as well get everything on the table," Purr said.

"What?"

"Mutt," John said. "I'm a clone."

I laughed out loud. "What?" I continued to chuckle. "John, you can't ruin this serious conversation like that. I can believe why these guys are trying to save world while keeping their reputation fresh, but I can't possibly believe that."

"Bill made a full-blooded copy of his brother when the fog came. Now that I know he is the reason for the rust fog, I guess he wanted me here to eliminate it. I've been taught to understand the mind of my dad. I've heard the last words of my father repeated by Bill thousands of times. *So Bright.* I think he was talking about the stars. But I failed Bill; I think he's going to kill us all."

"Wh-w-and now you tell me this! You're all just *full* of secrets! What the hell is the matter with all of you?! You know what, fuck this. Let me know when my bus trip is ready so I can try and make a person that I care for happy."

"Mutt, wait," John said, standing up after me. He stopped me at the door and whispered in my ear. "Please, we'll talk later, just let me find out where my uncle is, I promise you we will have a long talk."

I closed my eyes and nodded. "Where's Bill?"

"He's in critical condition." Set said.

In that very second that statement was made, John darted at the table and punched a clean hole through it. "WHAT?!"

"John, everything you said about the Owls thus far is true." Odradek's voice rattled as he stared at the open hole in the table, astounded by his strength. "Some are even working undercover. Listen, they tried to kill him while he was working on his project to save us."

"WHAT FUCKING PROJECT, ASSHOLE?!"

"That's secret, I'm so-"

"Fuck!" His face was so red with rage that the ice sculpture next to him began to thaw from the body heat. Little branches thinned out and broke off all over the table. "Now what?" He reached for his lock box. "Do you know what the fuck this thing is? He gave it to me as a piece of a riddle. It's a mystery; I've never found the damn key. And what for? So I can fully understand what my father taught him! If he dies, I will make damn sure the Owls get what they want."

"John, please. He's conscious. He just needs time." Odradek cautiously whispered. His breaths were becoming shallow. "Everything will be fine, I promise."

"Hmph," he marched past me to get to the door.

The mother stood up to stop John. "Boys, please." her voice was warm. "Let this be a goodbye gift from us, it's a note from Gleesty." I raced for it and swiped it from her hand.

Purr and Set stood up and bowed. "Let this be a farewell, perhaps we will cross paths again, with less tension."

I nodded, opened the door and walked down the hall with John behind me.

Thirteenth Chapter

I heard spits and snarls coming from John's mouth. He cursed until his tongue dried up and coughed hideously.

"Why have you never told me your secret? Am I really that much of a threat to you?"

"No, it's not that." His voice grew soft and fragile. "I was afraid of what you might think of me."

I laughed. "That's ridiculous."

"Not really. Think about it. You've never even bothered to befriend a clone, ever, because you despised them so much. So what if you knew that about me? You'd just be on with your way. Don't act like you're fine and dandy with it now. You used to mock us, ask me questions, like do clones dream? Do we have souls? Why do we have nipples? You laughed at how the replicants are sterile, and you laughed at the ones such as me because we weren't true-born."

"Yeah, I guess you're right." I laughed. "I'm sorry. I guess I do put out my hatred on anything that I don't understand."

"Whatever."

I looked back at the massive door. We both turned around and continued our way to our room. After a few turns, we almost completely forgot about our problems. And to mark it as a strange occasion, John grabbed my hand like a little child and walked with me. I felt like a parent helping his child across a busy street. "John, how did Bill manage to hide out? I mean, you guys were right under their noses when you moved near their HQ."

"He had plenty of money to keep a low profile," he said. "It's not as hard as you think."

He looked at me and smiled with the cheesiest words I've ever heard John say. "You're my only friend and I'm glad I am in this with you." It made me feel warm. I removed my hand from his, patted his back and lightly touched his head with mine. "Aren't we just the two most messed up cats?"

"The strangest anthropoids to ever dance."

"*Hey*", a voice was heard a few rooms away from ours. A door was open, and out popped a middle aged man glaring at us. "Hey, you there."

We walked over with curiosity. John nodded. "How do you do?"

"I have no friends." The man said. "No family. You two looked so happy. Can you spare a moment of your time?"

His face was swollen with sorrow. His words left us speechless. We had no idea what to say. "Is everything okay?"

"Come watch me die."

We stared at him. He was completely serious; there was no other way to explain it. His shivering lip was enough to convince us.

"Please, come inside."

We followed him inside. The lights weren't on, just hundreds of candles surrounding hundreds of white roses. I've rarely seen roses in general, and these healthy white ones really impressed me. "This is beautiful," I said.

"Thanks," he said. His voice was so calm. "My name is Baxter. I ran a florist just across the street."

"And you want to die?" John asked.

"Yes," he was on the verge of tears. "This is it." He sat down on his bed and grabbed a framed picture from the one table on the side of his bed. "I really wanted someone here with me. I don't want to be alone when it happens."

"I know that times are tough out there, but you should really have fai-"

"No!" He breathed in heavily, tears flowed down his face. "No, sorry but you don't understand. My friends have become those-fiends out there. I had a wife and a daughter, the same fate has fallen onto them. Do you know where they are now? Out there. And I rather die before becoming one of them."

"I'm sorry." I said.

"It's not your fault, mutant," he muttered. "It's been three days and I am in so much pain. I couldn't even protect my 9-year-old daughter. We were only across the street!" He sucked his breath in again and bit at his knuckle. "To watch your daughter disappear and become-*that*-was the most painful thing I have ever experienced. She was collecting her favorite flowers, these here, with her mother. We can only successfully grow them every few years. This year, we had so many grow. I normally can only get two dozen, but just look at them all! And I now know why I was so lucky this time around. These flowers are for her, for where she's going. My little girl just loved these." He couldn't hold his crying back anymore, and he waved us away from getting any closer to him.

"It's hard for everyone, sir." John said. "We've lost friends and family from all of this too. But the bright light is almost here. Please keep hope on your side."

"I've been damned too." He rolled up his right sleeve and showed us a bite mark. Our faces went white. "I went back there just an hour ago. I crept past the guards and managed to get inside my building. My wife was gone, but I remember hiding my daughter in the storage room after she was bitten. I went inside, and she was there. In her white dress, with the white roses. I got on my knees and opened my arms out to my child. She walked to me, and I swear I saw her smile." He turned his head and showed another bite mark on his neck. "I held onto her and accepted the pain." Baxter reached into his pocket and pulled out a handgun. "She bit my arm when I forced her back into the closet. I didn't have my gun at the time. I couldn't even end it for her."

John was trembling. He couldn't take anymore of this in one day. I looked at my hands and saw how much I was trembling.

"I have nothing else, and if I burn in hell, then so be it." He looked at both of us with a smile. "If you see a child in white, end it for me. I cannot face her again."

"What is your daughter's name, Baxter?" John asked. I wasn't sure if John was getting a kick out of this or if he was legitimately showing sympathy for the man.

He smiled. "Alice. It was Alice." Baxter raised the gun to his head after a series of coughs. "I have no interest in living as an abomination. I've done nothing wrong in my life, and I hope this one sin is forgiven."

"I'm so sorry, man." I had no idea what else to say. I couldn't stop him, it was no use.

"I don't know who you kids are, but thank you for coming here. I want you to alert the authorities after this, and be on your way."

We just stared.

"My favorite was the classic red rose." he rubbed the barrel of the gun on his temple. His smile was illuminated in the candle light behind the flowers. "I'll paint these red."

He pulled the trigger. The sound of the gun was almost as devastating as the slushgutter. Blood sprayed on the framed photo, on the walls, and on the white roses. We followed his orders and lead officers to his room. I have never felt so sorry for a person in my entire life.

I walked out of the room, leaving John behind. He apologized to the corpse of Baxter and followed me out to our bedroom.

Fourteenth Chapter

We both listened to the guards chatting about the body of Baxter across the hall. It was all too much for the both of us, and every time I stopped to think about what was going on, something else adds to the pressure. Then John started to laugh. They were not the same maniacal laughs that he let out while killing, or cracking a joke or any other type of jesting. The laughter coming from him was not the drumming *Ga-ha-ha-ha*, it was a squeaky, breathless giggle. I haven't heard this coming from him in a long time. It was his defense mechanism when he was under pressure, a common gesture that one could witness at funerals. I swear I only heard this laugh one other time: that dreadful day when I almost died from the overdose. I couldn't remember it until now, but those squeaks of his made that situation so much worse when he was cradling me in his arms while managing to get me to a hospital in a few minutes flat. My pupils were twitching after every yelp rippled through his larynx, out of his mouth and into my long, deranged ears.

He started calming down when I looked at him. His face was bright red. He bared his pointy teeth. His appearance resembled that of an angry fox. "Now Mutt, aha, listen to this. Listen to me here! You lovely scoundrel, you! Listening?"

"Yes, John."

"Alright," his laughing stopped as he reverted to a very calm, but serious John. "Remember the time we were walking out of your house, and we were going to my place to play a game when we were little? Before your parents were gone, I mean." He kept dishing his hands out like they were paintbrushes slashing away at an open canvas. "And we saw that person getting raped in an alleyway? She could barely make any noise, but we saw her. And we watched her eyes scream for help. The guy had his back turned, all we could see was his crazy looking high-end gas mask. He looked like a giant locust warrior summoned by Abaddon, ravaging its prey.

"And we kept watching, it was only for a few seconds. And we just walked away. We left her there to die. In our minds at that time, she was no different to us than a flower getting pissed on by a dog."

The last thing he said really hurt. It painted an image in my head really well. "Yeah, I remember." This was another memory that I could live without, and once again, one so terrible that I nearly forgot about. Today was a trip down the sewer hole at memory lane.

"We did nothing. Nothing! I did nothing because my entire life I misinterpreted what my uncle has been trying to teach me! You did nothing because, well, look at yourself. And man, remember the house fire a few blocks away from Wimsley's? Remember Wimsley?! He's dead! Gleesty killed him!"

"That's different, come on, where are you going with this?"

"Just remin-"

"No, there's a reason for it. You keep pouring lemon juice into the wound. What's on your mind?"

"I've really messed up! *I'm* really messed up! And now we start caring for others. Just *now*. Are we that selfish, or did we just realize something new? Look at Baxter. I know we didn't do anything there, but you know as well as I do that we felt something new towards other humans. Sorrow, sympathy, compassion." John continued preaching on top of his bed.

"It's time like these we learned that life is an anomaly." I was surprised at my words. "Am I becoming a giant raging pussy?"

"Times like *these?* We couldn't realize it when these people were in danger earlier?"

"What did they do when *we* were in danger, John?! We follow in with the rest of society! Are you really that blind?! They never lifted a finger to help us unless it had a good price on it! We aren't to blame, John."

"But we should feel that we are blamed for it."

"Why?"

"It makes us human. I know that just about everyone lost hope. And do you know why? They were trained to obey. Everyone alive right now does nothing but obey."

I shrugged at this. He wasn't making his point very clear to me, and I was concentrating on his flailing arms too much.

"Goresmith, uh, okay, let's say anyone who wants to take control, has taken control. They removed the basic needs for people by advancing on technology. They take our money. They give us exactly what we want. We just sit here, take our drugs to keep us happy, and listen when *they* tell us to do something. Nobody complains, they're too happy and lethargic to disagree. In short, let's say our lives have all necessities taken care of so well that if the rug was swept from under our feet, we'd fall and never get back up. They simply do not think for themselves."

"Yes, I understand. We've discussed this so many times."

"I know, but we need to recap on some things. Where was I? Oh yeah. Okay, so we are mindless drones."

"Zombies."

John froze. He never thought of it before. "Nice, Mutt. Profound. It's almost funny, too."

I smiled. I felt warm when he appreciated my input. I felt like a little boy being patted on the head.

"Anyway, these humans that we share our lives with do nothing but obey the Man. Some *may* rebel, or bring up some noise, until they realize they cannot leave the system. Then they shut up again. But now, something *has* affected the machine. A bigger machine. Bigger than Goresmith or any other corporation or government. So when the Man crumbles, the people go apeshit. They can't obey something that has crumbled!"

"Alright, so the system fails, and everyone loses faith."

"Yes. But we are not in the same spot as 'everyone.' I think we were subtly conditioned to survive this tragedy. We had a certain tool that steered us away from the normal lifestyle that has ended so many lives these past few days. We have a weapon!"

John started to lose his grip on the situation. I started to think that he was digging to deep in that head of his, but I kept following along. "The lock box?"

"Bill Strub."

I rolled my eyes.

"No, no think about it, Mutt. You ignored everything he's ever said. I misunderstood him until now!" He jumped off the bed, grabbed the book written by the man himself and waved it in front of my face. "He seeks a Tabula Rasa in *our* reality!"

"Okay, that's very nice."

"You aren't listening. Blank slate. Start over. He goes in circles with this all day."

"Yeah, I remember his need to cancel out the universe with the anti-black matter quark or whatever. He wanted to kill us. Now he wants to stop the zombies. I don't know, John, it's been going left and right and I can't keep up with it."

"Okay, let me try to straighten it out. He wanted to start over. But at first he thought there was only one way to do that. To completely erase everything so that something new happens. This was when he joined the Owls. A few of them from the Goresmith centers showed him to their way, which was to just plow everything over. Exterminate us all. That was about 20 years ago when the Morning Star thing occurred. He was pissed at how ugly the world looked when he saved us. And humans were so angry at how the world looked. And it made us all look bad. And the Owls knew that something like this would happen. Bill and them knew that there was the chance of the return of an apocalypse. Maybe not flesh-eating zombies, but they knew there was a greater power calling the shots here. And if they followed that agenda, waited until doomsday, then they win! We're plowed over as mindless drones until Earth itself dies out, so it could be reborn again."

It started to make sense now. "But are the Owls evil?"

"Evil really has nothing to do with it. They are indifferent on how it would happen, as long as it happens. Dadaists never have a solid plan. It forms as it goes along."

"So, why did Bill leave them?"

"He found another way. A new plan, it seems."

"So they tried to kill him because of it."

"Correct, they were probably scared that it would thwart the master plan. They fear it would make the world an even uglier place. You see?"

"Yes, I see."

"Owls just want the job done. They don't care about the casualties. Bill thinks he can go a different route. He doesn't want to sacrifice the entire human race for this ideal. Maybe that's why the Goresmith's came to him.

Perhaps he does know another way. I mean, come on. Shit, I've been so blind! Yow! He wants us to care, love and help each other out! Now I get it! I mean, I always *had* it, but you know what I mean."

And with that, a new laugh came out of John. This one's mood was bright and wonderful like a young bird singing underneath a bright yellow sun that we all longed to see. He reached into his front pocket and pulled out the lock box.

"This entire time, I was looking for a key. Bill gave me the option to cheat my understanding of everything. But at the same time, this must have been a trick test. I don't need anyone's help to understand life. I figured it out all by myself." He clasped it in his right hand, pulled it back and chucked it into the hard wall where it shattered into hundreds of pieces. "And hey, Gleesty had a second chance in life. Look what he did with it: He chose to help his friends."

I drove my attention away from the shattered lock box and suddenly remembered the note in my hand written by our handicapped friend. I opened it up as fast as possible, nearly ripping the damn paper into pieces. I tore a little bit of it, but not enough to prevent me from reading the document. I could barely make out the scribbles on the paper.

Mutt, John,

I am sure you know the truth of my family by now. Sorry, it is really hard writing this with my mouth. Look on the Bright side. I can fit inside of cars now. I cannot wait to see my great friends again. Never say die.

When I showed it to John he deflated with a sigh of relief.

I walked over to the shattered lock box.

"Mutt, what's the point?"

"Oh come on, I'll keep it to myself." I searched around the broken pieces to find a piece of paper the size of a half-dollar. I unfolded it and waved it to John. He shrugged and went to the bathroom. I examined every single word on the note at least 5 times to make sure I understood the message.

John. There is no key. There never will be.

Fifteenth Chapter

"What should we do before we ship out?" John was examining his naked body in the mirror. He had a great deal of wounds all over himself; sutured up with dental floss and super glue.

"I don't know," I said. "We can just relax the entire day. Tomorrow's going to be pretty heavy on us and everything will probably go wrong."

He nodded at this while flexing in the mirror. "Mhm, mhm. We can watch more residents blow their brains out, or sneak into the spot Gleesty is hiding, or even just meditate!"

There was a knock at the door.

"Please get that while I get dressed?" he walked into the bathroom and put his underwear on.

"Can't, I have two flat feet." I was far too comfortable to get up from the bed. My typical metal spring mattress paled in comparison to this duvet. It was some kind of liquid Tempur-Pedic. The bed post had a touch screen computer attached to it, so I browsed the internet for a few moments until I realized that people do this all day and it's a nasty habit to pick up. The average male masturbates 6 times a day because of this invention. I cannot let that happen to me. I am glad my parents were too poor to afford anything.

A long stick whizzed past my head and hit the bedpost, breaking the computer stand. John threw a hammer tacker at me.

"Asshole!"

"Get the door."

After several seconds of moaning and rolling around in the bed sheets, I walked over to the rumbling door. The knocking first was unrelenting and angry. I kept repeating w*ait, wait* until the knocking stopped. Gleesty was on my mind, and I was expecting him to jump through the door, laughing like an exhaust pipe as he tackled me down and tickled me until I let out a nay. My hopes were shut when I opened the door. Purr was standing there with a calm, humble look on his face.

"Sorry, I do get impatient," he said.

"Hey." Another *hey* came from behind me.

"What's up?"

"Perhaps we have come to a few misunderstandings." His voice kept crackling like a lost, shy child. What really perfected this image in my head was his artificial right eye. I had not noticed it at the dinner table. I watched its clockwise spiral as it scanned my brainwaves. This was not the first time I had an encounter with a cyborg eye. I've heard of the piece of technology before, and how it predicts emotions through body language. It still can't read minds, but it is a step closer to it. As I thought about it more, I came to the conclusion that he rarely spoke up because of that. He probably puts all his effort into understanding people just by watching them. Now, normally I am against our abusing of technology, but when we put effort in the right places (to serve the body and mind,) I am all for it. Recreational pleasure is the new disease that we all long to be stricken by. It is the new disease that everyone gets pissed off at you for having. One of Bill's sayings to technology was, "the only reason this was invented was so you could stick it up your ass. It's okay, I do it too."

"I support your opinion on my family to the fullest extent. I also wish you luck on your path. That's really why I'm here. To wish you luck. You two seemed very disgruntled on the helicopter subject. However, there is a real reason why we can't offer you one. My father is too shy to admit it, but our copters can only fit two people, driver included. My father has prepared for Judgment Day for two decades. He had thousands of theories on what might happen. He flushed billions into his research projects to push his technology into small simple machines for speed and rapid growth. He never expected it to be a sexually transmitted disease that acted like a sponge and lived off Negativium debris. All the while he gave up on the single person that could help him."

"I wonder why he would be shamed admitting that," John said with blatant sarcasm.

"Such bright and wonderful characters you both are. You are better off on the ground anyway. Oh, and once I get cleared tomorrow, I will be accompanying you with a copter. Don't mention this to my father, by the way. If anything goes wrong, maybe I can kamikaze myself into a gas station and cause hundreds of them to die." Purr winked at John with his fake eye.

"Thank you."

"Any questions, comments, comrades?"

"I'd like to see my uncle. Your family seems to be ignoring me a lot."

"Don't worry. We are taking you directly to him. Godspeed, degenerates." Purr opened the door and walked out.

"What a handsome young feller. Hey Mutt, did you check the news?"

"No, why? Did the gigglers sprout wings and start shooting lasers out of their asses?"

"No, but I caught an interview with an owl last night. She actually mentioned tabula rasa. Everything has been confirmed. The zombies started chanting again. Real dramatic stuff. And the reporter himself even muttered, 'there are no atheists in foxholes.' Everyone is turning to their original faiths. They want to repent!"

"Does that mean they are against cloning?"

"Considering that all faiths and creeds are joining together to try and fight this, I really don't think so! Everyone has put their differences aside to *live*. We have zombies and Owls versus humans and clones! And really ugly mutants!"

"I wonder what's going on in Heaven and Hell."

"Apocalypse beach party!"

"What?"

"No, really. The Owls are throwing an apocalypse beach party."

"I hate you so much."

"Now I've been thinking..."

"Ah, fuck. What did I tell you about doing things like that?"

He laughed. "Mutt, are we meeting in heaven or hell?"

"Huh? Well, Heav-"

"Nope. While I commend these people for restoring their faith, I'd much rather be with the interesting people down there."

"Eh, uh, okay, John. Let's decide to go to hell. I don't think anyone has ever purposely chosen that. Whatever, so, how are we meeting when we get there?"

"Let's climb the highest mountain there and meet up with everyone."

"Everyone?"

"Yeah, Gleesty, and, you know, Bill."

"Alright, John, so, what happens if there are two mountains equally as high?"

"Good God, Mutt! Okay, the water fount-"

"There's no water in hell, chief."

"Let's build a fountain anyway!"

"John, you know as well as I do that I will get the water fountain confused with the lava fountains in the eternal hellfires."

"Okay, smartypants, where?"

"Hmm." I scanned the room looking for clues. My eyes locked on to the digital clock on the dresser. "We will meet at the biggest clock tower."

"Clocks! Bill *loves* clocks! And if there isn't one, we'll just build it!"

"I don't think they will let us."

"Demons need to know the time too, so I think they will let this pass. We can even put a sun dial there!"

"I think you're missing the point."

"With a water fountain on it. It's always 3:15 p.m. in Hell anyway."

From the looks of it, John wasn't leaving the bed. This was my chance. I headed for the door, expecting him to say something once I reached the doorknob. He kept quiet, still, staring at the ceiling muttering numbers. This math thing with John is fascinating, but I could only take so much. The numbers drip out of his mouth and form rancid memories that seep into my head. He used math to calm himself, to stimulate himself. Depending on what equation he said, his eyes would sparkle or dim. Right now it looked like was trying to lull himself into a slumber.

"Hey, I'm going out." I opened the door and got one hoof out into the hallway.

"Wait."

I shut my eyes and cringed. "Yeah?"

"Why?"

"I'm running away. It's time I join the wild spirits. I will always be in your heart. Whistle if you're in danger."

He laughed. "Need some time with the normal human race?"

"Yeah, you're too much sometimes."

"No problem. I'm going to watch the news."

"Keep me updated. I'll be back in a few hours."

I am not sure why I thought getting away from him was going to be difficult. After a few steps out in the hallway, my stomach started to rumble. Going back to John was a bad idea, so I decided to head over to the public cafeteria.

The place was packed. There was so much noise going all around. Parents with their kids arguing about taking extra cupcakes, kids pissing themselves in the lunch line, adults pissing themselves because the opiates they received completely shut out their natural bodily functions. It was almost like my old high school eatery.

The room was twice the size of a basketball court, enough leg room for anyone that preferred to eat here rather than their tiny abode in the building. Everyone still had the look of shock on their faces from the aftermath. Some kept their eyes glued to one of the four televisions. Not a single blink. Small conversations took place. I could hear a few people cry- I noticed few people weeping in the palms of their scabbed hands. Everyone was waiting for the good news to roll in. We want rain. That was the topic of discussion. Where is our rain? If it rained, the irradiated acid needles could pierce through the skulls of the infected and end most of our worries.

I waited in line, browsing the various foods they had. I picked up a cheeseburger. The first time Bill Strub saw me eat one of these he called me a cannibal. Funny guy.

I grabbed some orange juice and some soup and I was all set. I wandered around with my tray until I found an open table. I sat down and started to eat. There were a few pretty girls around, but nothing at all like Mary. I was hoping that one of these dirty, bruised girls could be her clone. I searched for Mary's sickeningly long eyelashes. I thought about some clues that could help me identify the clone. Nothing. Mary was perfect in my eyes. Not a blemish, wrinkle or scar could I remember from her naked body. I looked around the room: ugly, saddened faces. How hard could it be finding a perfectly sculpted figure? No, that's not good enough. I had to dig deeper. Her personality; the way she spoke, walked and breathed- so many things stand out from other people. It was just different, like she was from another time. I had to find a drafted clone that was under the heavy influence of Mary.

"Mutant S. Barrows?"

The image of Mary deteriorated in my mind. I turned around and saw an old, gray man standing behind me in awe. His glasses were resting on the very edge of his nose. His face had mild wrinkles near his mouth and around his eyes. "Happy" wrinkles from smiling too much. I nodded and smiled at the stranger.

"Mutant," he said. "I'll be fucking damned!" He slapped his knee hard and shook his head.

"Well damn, you're probably the happiest person I've seen in the past 2 years," my smile grew wider. "That says a lot, especially right now. Uh, you know my full name. Rare. I'm flattered, but call me Mutt."

"I'm Charlie Sutters. Shyeet. I am surprised that you're still alive! No offense boy! Haha!"

His happiness brightened me up. I couldn't help but laugh with him. "Who the fuck are you, Charlie?"

"Ahahaha!" his laugh was so soothing. People looked up from their soaked hands and cracked a smile. He just lightened the place up. His smile faded. "Your parents-uh-"

I interrupted. "Sorry," my smile went away as well. "I don't want to hear their names."

"Understood. Well, your father's father, Gregori, what do you know about Gregori Barrows?"

This really caught my attention. I knew very little about my grandfather. "My dad seldom ever spoke about him. Oh, please sit down." He took a seat at the other end of the table. His red and black plaid shirt smelled like tobacco.

"I was great friends with your grandpa. Let me start from the beginning. When he immigrated to this country, he worked in the toughest, back-breaking jobs that this place had to offer. He loved kicking his own ass. That crazy fucker ate barbed wire and shit out yarn. Oil rigs, mining, blacksmithing, welding, slaughterhouses, he did it all. When he was 45, sometime after your dad sold most of his property, he sailed away in this decently sized yacht that he built all by himself. Man, oh man, I was just traveling around when I saw him on the docks. And I just went with him. The half angry/half relieved look in his eye carried me around the seas for years.

The boat, a damn beautiful boat, had micro-greenhouses, various weapons and all sorts of technology to stay involved with what was going on in the world. I remember asking him why he wanted to leave everything that he had here in the states. He just said, 'fuck it' and went." Charlie flicked his hand into the air. "And we just went. I was fleeing from the war, haha! Then, the rust happened-you happened. We really had no idea what to think. And don't think bad about it, he longed to meet you, buddy."

This was amazing. The only thing my dad ever mentioned about my grandpa was that he was selfish and never cared about a thing. It could be true, but he sounded like a self-made man that I longed to be. My father was the selfish, greedy asshole that took an opportunity to wrong someone to make money.

He stared at my ears. "Hah, those must get all the ladies!"

I ignored his comment, "so, what happened?"

"Oh, God, we drifted. Our first trip before we had to dock was 3 years. The only reason we *had* to dock was because of this industrial catastrophe. So we left the boat at a spot in Jersey, he went to visit his son, to see if he was still alive. Found out about the farm, went to it, saw you, and cried. He wasn't ashamed of you, boy. He was ashamed of that damn son of his. He wanted to just take you away with us, but your dad said you needed medication or you would get sick and die. I'm certain that's bullshit."

"It is. Then what happened?"

"We got back on and left again. We lived on the sea for almost 25 years. We just went from place to place to try and forget everything. And then, well, I was tired. I came back here a few months ago. Now this shit happens."

"My grandpa is still alive?"

"Greg is sailing. Lucky guy, I mean, we're lucky to be alive right now but that guy had the right idea. The pollution isn't nearly as bad in the ocean because of the extra moisture. Sure, we have to fish a little deeper, but we were safe out there. I really am not sure what happened to your grandma, he never spoke much about her."

"She was hanging around my father until she called it quits too. She just went down south, my dad once said she got in trouble, but I really don't know if she died or if she's in jail or wh-"

"This is too much for me, haha. Let's just stick with the present now. Well, what's your story, Mutt?"

I sighed. "I'm looking for someone, but so much has been happening that I can't even stick to my main plan."

"A girl?"

"Yeah, I'm a pathetic loser looking for a complete stranger. "I'm really smart and cool."

"Hm."

"I'd explain the situation to you, but it would probably make it a lot worse."

He laughed. "Would you rather sit around here and wait for something to happen?"

I sat there in silence trying to analyze the people around me in my peripheral vision.

"I maimed my friend because of her. Well, not *her*, but her parent-thing. The one I'm looking for is a clone, her parent sent me out to find her before she was struck down."

Charlie shook his head violently and waved away the thoughts. "Before you say anything else," he reached into his pocket for a pen and grabbed one of my napkins off the table. He wrote a phone number. "Let's say we all managed to survive this pickle. This is your grandpa's number. You probably wouldn't get through to him right now, honestly. He's too far and the signal is too muffled. But listen, try calling every now and then, maybe, one day he'll be close enough to the shores." He wrote down another number. "That's mine, well, if my place is still standing. Every now and then your grand-dad will contact me for small chat. Want to give me yours in case he does?"

A piece of the napkin was ripped off and handed to me. I nervously wrote the number down with poor handwriting. To me, it was like signing the Declaration of Independence. "My apartment, if it is still around. This really means a lot to me. Thanks for finding me, really. This was just what I needed."

Charlie smiled and shook his head once more. "Boy, you just stand out so much." He bobbed his head up and down. "It's not just the ears. Those eyes of yours, kid. You just look so innocent. Well, then again, you almost killed your friend for a girl, eh?" He roared with laughter.

"What would you do in my situation?" My hooves were digging into the wooden floor and making hideous marks on the finish. The scraping noise strangely calmed me down.

"Put it this way. Let's say you stayed here with my old balls, never challenged yourself out there. Years from now when this shit blows over, will you regret never closing *that* door? Would it haunt you?"

"Yes," I said. "Things like these that really affect me. I mean, I've gotten this far, right?"

"And what is your biggest fear right now?"

My writhing leg halted. My stomach began to twitch as the inside of my throat felt like it was housing a nest of slugs.

"-Euh- Uh. Just, failing I guess." I gave a generic answer. I couldn't think. I had to wrap the conversation up. Of all the times, I had to run into junk sickness now. However, I was impressed with myself that I lasted so long. The adrenaline probably kept me in line. Charlie watched my face, which was probably pale white now, and slightly tilted his head.

"You alright, Mutt?"

"Yeah, yeah," the sweat between my fingers sickened me, it just felt so wrong. "I just arrived here, I'm just exhausted."

"Ah, well then. Go get some rest. I'll probably just hang out at that recreational center for some chess."

I nodded. He bought it. Another few minutes and I'll be coughing up a lung. He grabbed my hand, slapped the back of it and smiled. "It's a shame this was so short, but I think we're going to have plenty of time to talk. If not here, then in the next world."

After a few steps out into the hall, I bolted out and into my room and vomited in a waste basket a few inches away from the door. John turned away from the television.

"You had the fish, didn't you?"

Sixteenth Chapter

Fifteen hours of vomit, shit, goosebumps and chills. By the time the ride was prepared I was completely exhausted from the sickness. Those 15 hours were not slow, I remembered all the torment. I recall John carrying me to a detox clinic inside of the building. The detoxification did the trick, even though it was probably the most unpleasant thing that I have ever experienced.

Now, there were several different methods to get clean. John, as well as the doctors, offered me meth to wean myself. I kindly declined and went for the cold turkey. When they saw I was suffering too much, they rammed tubes inside of me and flushed what needed to be flushed out. I am glad they did; if I waited the entire thing out, all of my plans would have fallen through. Yesterday was probably the worst time to start over in life. At least that step was over.

And John hummed. John hummed when the nurses stuck me on the wheelchair after that traumatizing purification process. John hummed when he wheeled me into the halls. John's hums were slowly dripping into my half-distorted mind. His echoing music warped my vision into oily glazed swirls and this miserable pseudo-acid trip was complete.

I vaguely recall him stealing a handful of syringes and chemicals from the clinic. When I tried to tell the nurses, nothing but slurs and drool emerged from my mouth.

Purple and black blotches of ink were all that I could see while I was taken to the giant truck. I had my mind set on going, no matter what my condition was. I constantly repeated "Nuwuark" until they understood what I wanted to do.

"Mutt, just take this shot."

"Nurrrghh."

"I'm loading you up in the truck now. Can you see yet? The truck is pretty beat up looking. Not like the photo. Quite impressive nonetheless. It has three turrets on the roof!"

"Frrmen."

"Yes, yes, Mutt. Furr-men."

More slurs, distorted colors and warped sounds for the next twenty minutes, until I passed out momentarily. Another twenty minutes went by, and I was surrounded by about a dozen soldiers in full black armor and masks to boot. Everything was restored; no more disoriented senses. John must have given me a shot while I was sleeping. The soldiers, in reinforced Kevlar and riot masks, stared at me in silence. John was sitting in one of the seats that surrounded the inside of the truck. I was in the middle, which had nothing more than a floor. Scanning the area, I noticed that there were half a dozen television screens, all fastened on the wall. Cameras strapped on the truck were used to monitor the blind spots.

The truck had yet to move. Perhaps they were all waiting for me to regain consciousness. John clapped excitedly when I started tapping my hooves on the cold, hard ground. A few soldiers clapped. From what I can tell, it was 9 male soldiers and 3 females. Probably all clones.

I glanced around, got up from the floor and identified John. "What happened?"

"Don't worry about it. You didn't keep us waiting that long."

One soldier got up from his seat and giggled. "You should have heard what you said in your sleep, bro!"

I looked at the one that spoke, "as you were, soldier."

"Which one of my fucking daft cunts spoke?!" a roar came from the back of the truck. One of the soldiers got up and walked towards the one that laughed. "Did I *not* say that if someone spoke, I will ram my boot into their fucking chest?"

The "leader" had a gold triangle badge attached to his chest. One of the female soldiers had a red one. Another male soldier also had a red one. The 9 others all had white marks. All were most likely different ranks. I watched the gold-badge one ram his boot into the white-badge soldier. Everyone sat down and stayed silent, except for the two red-badge soldiers.

The leader saluted me, picked me up from the floor and apologized for his "incompetent warrior."

"Are we still in-"

"Yes we are, sir," his voice mellowed out after his outrage. "We have about an hour drive ahead of us because of the blockages. We should be able to just go straight through everything with no problem. Isn't being a V.I.P. nice?"

Bleeps were coming from a computer, then from the soldiers helmet. "Excuse me, uh, Mutt, was it? Call me Sergeant Ray. Behind me are my two specialists, Lala and Sol." Ray waved his finger around his head, quickly pointing to the white soldiers and saying their names carelessly. "Bill, Mitch, Nina, Alexandra, Gunther, Truth, Drew, Nick and Ryan. Privates. You and John will be our guests on this little mission of ours. Let's get some facts straight. I'm not a nice guy. This will be the nicest I will act today. My mission is to bring the supplies in the other cart safely to the station in Newark and to bring you guys there alive."

I nodded. "Yes, Sergeant," my jaw was still shaky, it was still difficult to speak. I had a minor headache, but I was at least able to function properly.

"Good, good. Sol and Lala have been assigned to be your personal body guards. You follow them." John and I both glanced at the masked Specialists, who nodded to us, walked over and sat beside me and John. Sol, the male, rested his gun on his lap and offered John a cigarette. Lala, who seemed fascinated by my appearance, stroked my ear and scooched with me to a seat next to John.

"Sol, Lala, can I rely on both of you here and now?"

Sol let out a roar of a reply, which made my ears ring. Lala softly muttered "Yes."

"Good. Mutt, John, they are still new to instructions. They all are. These clones have just passed their tests. But don't you worry. My specialists have completed the exams with flying colors. "If I hear *any* privates giving *any* sort of input during this ride without my permission...I will fucking kill you. Simple as that. I am going to fucking kill you. Got that?"

"Yes Sir!" The echo burst my eardrums. I moaned in pain.

The Privates would stay quiet for the rest of the ride. They pointed their guarded heads towards all the monitors. After a few seconds, and with an OK from Ray, we drove off into the chaos. Ray and Sol kept a conversation with John and I, while Lala just looked, breathed and giggled.

"You two are legends at this point. Anyone capable of surviving in the red zone for three days cannot possibly be a weakling," Sol said. "The Goresmiths took great pleasure in talking about you for some reason. Probably because of that mad scientist of yours."

Ray grunted. "Sol, shut it."

John looked at them in shock.

"John, it is for security purposes." Ray glanced at his white-badge soldiers and whispered to us. "One of my privates was an owl that volunteered to fight with us. A fucking clone. These guys were nobodies until *this* happened. Incredible. Anyway, we got too comfortable around the private, and we almost lost his uncle. Now let's not talk about this again. We've informed the privates here that both of you are just looking for your parents."

We heard the large gates swing open.

I looked at Ray. "How have the zombies been around here?"

Lala giggled. "Oh, my."

Sol let out a sigh of relief. "You haven't heard? They've left this area for the time being. They now travel in large clusters. Depending on what they are."

"Are?" John asked.

"Gigglers, leapers, ticklers, mutants. Gigglers are the laughing assholes. Leapers are the pox-leper-jumping assholes. Ticklers are these crying children with overgrown spiked rib cages. Don't let them hug you. And, mutants. Fucking mutants. There's a handful of them and they're like, the leaders of the swarm. That's why we want to lock down all non-infected mutants."

"Have you fought any mutants?" John asked.

"Thank God, no. This vehicle has been taken through things, including bridges, but not a mutant."

About 5 minutes down the road we heard it. The laughing, the screeching and the crying. We watched on the monitors as many of them were pulverized by the vehicle. Some Privates shot at the zombies through the open slots of the vehicle, "to test the waters." The guns they were all wielding were semi-automatic rifles. I suppose these were the best things to use against them. Sol got onto a turret and blew a great sum of them to smithereens.

John pulled our backpack of supplies. Opening the bag, he reached inside and handed me my gun. The magazine remained with a single bullet.

John looked at Sol. "So, how exactly does this thing go through a bridge?"

Sol laughed. "Okay, it only happened once. The bridge was already fucked up, so we just plowed through what was left of it. This is a big fucking machine, so we normally just take the long way and ignore paths like that. But the driver got bored, I guess."

"Helicopter behind us," John said, pointing to one of the monitors. It could barely be seen through the fog, but it was definitely a copter.

"Ah, nice, Purr's here," Ray said. "Weird family, let me tell ya. Even with all the power they have, they still demand to be in the battle. Respectable."

The family, from my understanding, always seemed like they owed a debt to the world. Perhaps that's what drives them to these impulses.

Sol and Ray joined the privates in their target practice. When they reached areas where the fog wasn't too heavy, they went for long range with their cannon-turrets. They laughed as their bullets liquefied zombie heads. John asked to try, but his request was denied by Ray. Ray seemed to have a good idea that John was too reckless.

Lala started a small conversation with me. Her voice was soft and put a lot of emphasis on every word that past her lips.

"So you're all here just to find that...man?" She whispered. "That's what everyone said. I am happy people still find value towards family. Most of us are selfish people. Then again, your uncle is quite important."

I smiled at her, "I'm really just looking for a friend. It's a shot in the dark that I will find her there."

"Is she a clone?"

I nodded.

"Well," she giggled. "If she is there, then she is most definitely worth your time. The facility in Newark is where all the top soldiers and high class clones go."

This made me smile. I thought about how perfect Mary was. Someone in the place must know Mary. Her name, at least. I am certain that I can find the name of her clone and meet her.

"I'm going to join the boys and girls. Enjoy your friend here." She cautiously walked over to where the other soldiers were, sat down, and started firing."

John looked at me and smiled. "Since when did females speak to you?"

"You seem to be enjoying yourself today," I told John.

"Of course, I just took some opiates." He revealed all the syringes and containers full of fluids.

"What are the others?"

"Who knows? I just take them. I was bored and this truck goes quite slow."

"You're sick in the head," I sighed at him.

The rest of the ride was quiet up until the end. Because it is difficult to reach a radio signal, we managed to get a forwarded message from Purr via helicopter. The boar mutant that Odradek introduced to me earlier managed to snap out of his slumber. He burst through the walls and ran off to our direction. The way Purr said everything made it seem like it was after us. Everyone cursed, asked Purr if everyone was fine. For the most part, yes. The gate must be prepared before zombies find the opening and pour in. Luckily, the survivors collected themselves and helped support the soldiers that defended them. This was astounding. I couldn't help but think that this was Charlie's doing. So many depressed people could not possibly bother to lift a finger. I expected them to rampage, worry, cry and attempt to mutiny. It gave me more hope in humans.

"Purr, do they have the boar marked? Anything? Didn't they put a fucking tracking device on it before? Or a bomb in case it did flee?" Ray was panicking. He took his helmet off, the first soldier to reveal themselves to me. He looked exactly how I imagined him. Shaven head, a strong jaw with a thick nose that looked like it was carved out of wood.

Purr's voice was heard over the radio. "We do have a tracking device on it. We're on it. We're sending reinforcements for you just in case. Guard the middle of the vehicle. If it does get to you, it will strike there."

"Fuck. FUCK." Sol threw his helmet off, but then quickly cooled down. Sol looked a little different from other clones. He had some unique body modifications from the looks of it. The canines in his mouth were much longer than any normal human. His green hair, light orange skin and pointed ears surprised me. I have heard of a few clones that were modified to look different before they were born, but not one up close. He had a primitive fantasy appearance to him.

"Fuck it, I don't care anymore. I'm going to have fun. Get the explosives ready." Sol grabbed the controller to the turret and growled hungrily. A few minutes past. He stared at his monitor and cursed again.

"What?" Lala asked.

"Look at that."

"The mutant? Already?"

"No, not *that* mutant, take a look at this." Everyone rushed to his side of the vehicle and stared at the monitor. "Holy shit."

It was the size of a car. Heads, arms, legs, stomachs, all of it emerged from this swarming mound of flesh. It slurred and moaned and crawled like a lethargic cat. This particular zombie managed to merge with several others. It looked absolutely disgusting. The soldiers agreed to stop the vehicle and try to kill it.

John objected. "How far are we from the destination?"

One of the privates answered. "It's two streets down, let's just have some fun."

"What should we call this thing?"

"The legion," John said. "I wonder if there are others."

"Probably, let's fuck it up." Sol giggled.

They opened fire at it. The orchestra of bullets pierced the purple swollen veins of the mutant. It made a sweet humming sound that turned into an incredibly high-pitched shriek.

Sol had not fired the turret yet. Lala took it from his hands and fired a single shot at it. The bullet hit a car next to the legion and exploded. It knocked out a quarter of the beasts flesh, making it howl. Lala ripped her helmet off in satisfaction and let her hair flutter.

"Die sickies, die!" John screamed.

And then she said the two words that I fell in love with. The words that made my adventure worth dying for:

Fucking checkmate!

It echoed in my heart and brought me back to the night Mary and I slept together. I looked at Lala, and she looked at me, confused at the look on my face. Pink hair, sky blue teeth, blue freckles that glowed like little distant stars. Her appearance was most satisfying. Mary's clone was right here next to me the entire time. John's mouth swung open. He waited for me to say something, afraid that his personal theory was too good to be true. And she was waiting for me to say something. And all of the soldiers waited for me to say something. The look on my face was probably horrific.

I blinked, closed my mouth and opened it again. My chest felt like it was caving in. "Mary sent me." That was all I could squeeze out of my lungs. But it was enough. The look on her face was enough to tell me that everything was going to be okay. I kept my promise to Mary. John looked like he was about to cry. The soldiers, extremely confused, went back to monitor the legion. The ugly zombie started singing again.

I watched as Lala slowly walked towards me. The series of monitors, perfectly aligned with her head, showed nothing but explosions and blood splatter adorning her sides. Even the undead were watching Lala as she walked over to embrace me. Music was heard. The sounds of trumpets, I swear, could be heard. It was an astounding moment. The beautiful sounds of the trumpets grew louder, like there was more and more of them. Lala still has yet to say a word. We kept our eyes locked now. She was three feet away when my longing for her was shattered. Every step she took the background noises grew louder.

In my peripheral vision, I watched a giant zombie tackle the vehicle over and knock the truck to its side. We were all thrown around. Screams and cracking metal joined in with the wailing trumpets. Most of the security cams were shattered, except for three. One showed nothing but a building. The second camera showed the Owls on the rooftops playing the trumpets like mad angels. They played the trumpets as the legion sang. The third camera showed the most terrifying thing that I ever witnessed. It was a gigantic white horse.

"Come! Come!" shouted the Owls to the horse mutant. "Come!" the beast itself shouted to his army.

Lala's fingertips kissed mine when we were pummeled to the ground. The noises grew louder. The number seven was all I could think about.

Seventeenth Chapter

"And I saw, and behold a white horse. Mutt, the seals are breaking. Something has been awakened. The Owls are now angels. It is our time." John's words were frightening. Everyone else in the tilted vehicle grunted and recuperated. I was resting in Lala's arms, both of us watching the monitor of the horse attempting to break inside. It huffed wildly at the large metal box in front of it, trying to break through. The Owls continued playing their trumpets and yelling. Everyone was too scared to speak.

"Everyone keep quiet," Ray whispered. "Reload your rifles. We're not going out without a fight."

I got up from Lala's arms and tried to speak. She instantly pressed her lips against mine and said, "I didn't think she meant you literally *were* a jackass. Oh my god. Where is she?"

I whispered back to her. "Out there. One of them. She sent me to find you."

"Soldier," Ray whispered to Lala. "No time for that now. We gotta-"

John interrupted. "Then another came out, a fiery red one. Its rider was given power to take peace from the earth and to make men slay each other. To him was given a large sword."

"John, shut the fuck up!" Ray yelled.

By the time he finished those last words, we heard another "COME!" as we were flung forward by another powerful force. And there it was, a giant goat covered in blood on the third monitor alongside the horse. He managed to pierce a hole big enough at the rear of the mobile for me to put my head through. We all sat and watched the two golems through this hole. Behind them were the lesser "demons" watching their leaders strike.

Everyone was panicking now. Sol grabbed the radio and started screaming for Purr to help. Purr attempted to calm him, but that went in vain. "Just fucking do something!"

"Hang on for another minute, I promise you that you will be just fine." Purr said.

"That's bullshit, Purr! Your thin-skinned family fucked us!"

And another blast. This time, it hit us in the center of the vehicle. The impact punched another hole in the floor, slightly bigger than the first one. The two privates leaning on the wall were killed instantly by the blow. It ripped their helmets off and bent their necks to their shoulders. The privates screamed when they realized two of their teammates were gone. And through that hole we saw the enormous boar, covered in filth, unchained and raging. With another howl from the Owls, "Come!"

"When the *fuck* did Charlotte's Web get so fucking twisted?!" A private yelled.

"A measure of wheat for a penny, and three measures of barley for a penny, and see thou hurt not the oil and the wine," John muttered.

"Hang on! Hang on!" We could hear from the radio. Everything was happening too fast to react.

Ray threw a grenade, followed by a smoke bomb, followed by a flash bang. "Soldiers, fire at whatever the fuck!"

And they all followed in. They poked their guns through the slots and the punctured holes and fired recklessly outside. John and I realized that the air filter wasn't working enough to keep the fog out of the truck, so we grabbed the helmets from the soldiers and equipped them. John took his off and laughed. "The fuck is this thing going to do?" He threw the helmet at me and grabbed one of the guns from the dead soldiers. "Mutt, grab the other and join me." I nodded in agreement and followed his orders.

Thirty seconds of firing and everyone had to reload. Then, a horn half the size of me went through the vehicle and cut the remaining privates in half. It wounded Sol's leg, but Lala, Ray, John and I were lucky enough to avoid it. The fourth creature's horn curved upwards like a can opener and peeled an opening for the zombies to see. We were now wide open. The five of us watched in horror as we witnessed how great and powerful the final zombie was. A bull-no, a minotaur. It stood 25-30 feet tall. Aside from the horns, the hooves and the bull-like face, it looked like a giant human, unlike the others. It was pale, bloody and dirty. And then it taunted us with a roar, "Come!"

The four zombie beasts stood 50 feet from us. Behind them were thousands of zombies. Ticklers, gigglers and leapers. All just watching us. Watching me. The horse stood about 20 feet in length. The goat, the shortest of the bunch, was about 15 feet. The boar was matched with the horse. And then we had the hulking giant, standing behind them like a leader. All of them on their hind legs, waiting for us.

Ray stood up from the ground and watched them breathe as they slowly chanted "come." "I've read the bible, and I thought Cherubs were..."

"No," John said. "These are not beings from the holy light. They are evil. They are mocking God. This was all controlled by Lucifer. This is his interpretation of the apocalypse. And in front of us are the False Horsemen."

How long, Sovereign Lord, evil and false, until you judge the inhabitants of the earth and avenge our blood?

The Owls began chanting with their companions.

A grenade whizzed past us and blew up in front of the zombies. The 144,000 zombies (I can only guess) behind them roared. The trumpets continued. They all chanted "Come!" as they laughed their lifeless laughs. The legion had disappeared. And the remaining five of us did nothing but shiver. They watched us, waiting to see what we could possibly do.

John spoke to me. "Mutt, you had one bullet in that gun of yours."

"Yes," I said.

"There were three bullets originally, weren't there?"

Tears fell from my eyes. I still answered him. "Yes."

"That last bullet was for you, wasn't it? The other two are in the skulls of your parents."

I nodded, shaking violently.

"And now what? Will you use it on yourself? Will you turn away from the light and *die?*" John was shouting. He cried with me, but with a smile. He inhaled the fog and exhaled it through his nose. "I need to know if you are my true friend. Are you ready to die? Are you going to pull that handgun out and blow your brains right here and *fucking die?!*"

I raised the rifle and pointed it at the mutants. "No, John! Never! Never say die!"

Lala, Sol, Ray, and John all looked at me and nodded. I removed my helmet and smiled at them, revealing my tears.

We heard something on the roof, we prepared our rifles. Suddenly, we heard it say "Amen." We looked up.

A giant hulking metallic phantom leaped up into the air, higher and higher, matching the height of a building. It was too dark to see it. Purr's helicopter could be heard over the hissing of the zombies. The trumpets stopped. The gigantic insect crashed down in front of the horse. The impact caused an earthquake and a cloud of dust and smoke. We all collapsed from the explosion. We got up and watched the smoke clear.

And there appeared Gleesty, standing beside a headless horse in silence. His body was modified into something I did not think would ever be possible. His legs were a shining metal; giant pistons in his heels, several pneumatic tubes in his shins, along with odd looking purple orbs where his kneecaps should be. His torso boggled my mind. More metal, more sensors, and near his thighs was a gyroscope. His arms were still gone. There were now four other limbs in their places. Two of them were gigantic blades, both about six feet in length. Below these blades were two robotic "arms." He extended them out like a praying mantis, and underneath the wrists unfolded two more thin swords. His head was encased in this clear liquid helmet. It hovered on top of his shaved head.

"That is," John choked. "The single most badass fucking thing I have ever seen in my entire life. He's like a cyborg-Viking!" John started to drool all over his chest.

"Our angel has arrived!" Lala dropped her gun and clapped with delight.

When the gigglers, leaper and ticklers stood up from the earthquake, they examined my metallic hero. They took a step back. The damn plague took a step back. It started to rain. It was a light drizzle, but enough to cool my body down. The smell of sulfur arrived at our noses. The insects began to fly away, and the birds followed them.

We all heard Gleesty laugh. "There will be no more delays! I am Alpha and the Omega! Who is, and who was, and who is to come..."

The three remaining beasts roared. Gleesty bent his knees, jumped forward and kicked the gigantic minotaur in the chest, sending him flying into zombies, and crashing into a building that tumbled on top of it.

"Fuck, wait, no, this is terrible!" John shouted.

We all looked at John, who was anxiously searching through his injection refills for something.

"John, excuse me?" Sol asked. "We might have a chance to live here!"

"No! No, no, no!" He started to stomp his feet. He grabbed a container filled with strange blue liquid. "Ray, what's in this?"

"Uh, what?"

"What the fuck is in this?!"

"Hyper-Amyl Nitrate."

"And this?" John showed him a pink fluid.

"Dude, that stimpack fluid has been banned for twenty years, where'd you get it?"

"And this?" John showed a yellow liquid.

"Horse aphrodisiac, I really hope you aren't planning on taking those..."

"HE'S GOING TO GET THE HIGH SCORE! HOW CAN I COMPARE TO THAT?!" John was fuming as Gleesty shredded dozens of zombies by the second. His visceral whirling blades spun and twisted as his body acted like a contortionist. He was moving at an incredible speed; he would often scrape up about 20 zombies, fling them into the air, land on the ground, jump back up and slice them all in half in one shot. The goat and the boar chased after the warrior.

"He's getting, like, 500 points right now! That horse was like 50 alone! I'm only at 2,300 after the slushgutter!" John put a quarter of each liquid into the syringe and went for his jugular.

Sol yelled, "No! In the anus! Not the Ne-"

"GGGUUURRRAHHHFFFFFAAAHHHHH!" John fell to the floor and convulsed violently like a contemporary Mr.

Hyde. His skin crawled as we watched in horror when all of the vessels in his eyes burst to give off a brilliant angry red color. His wheezing disturbed the four of us. John rose up and started singing. "BLESSING, AND GLORY, AND WISDOM, AND THANKSGIVING, AND HONOR, AND POWER, AND MIGHT, BE UNTO OUR GOD FOR EVER AND EVER! KITTENS!"

We all kept repeating "oh my god" as he grabbed two rifles and leaped out of the wreckage.

"I am warlord Jesus Christ!" he shouted as he raised the guns into the air. He spun around, attempting to imitate Gleesty as he pulled both triggers, firing aimlessly into the air. Several barely missed us. "John, no!"

But John was lost. There he was, performing a psycho ballad in a tuxedo with two rifles. A few leapers attempted to grab at him, but he managed to fight them off quite easily. Gleesty flung the goat to John's direction, where the giant mutant got up and roared at the raging psychopath. John laughed and fired directly into the goat's neck until it fell to its knees. My friend dropped the guns and managed to leap up and grab the goats head. He yanked on it for several seconds until he ripped it off! John started showering in its blood until the body lay lifeless on the ground.

"No fucking way," Sol said. "He just killed War for 50 points."

John continued laughing hysterically as he pulled the skull and brains out of the head and put it on like a mask. He realized how terrible it smelled and wore it like a crown instead. He reloaded one gun, started to bah like a goat, and continued on his killing spree.

"Should we make a run for it? We're what, two streets away?" I asked.

Sergeant Ray reloaded his gun and pointed to the left. The zombies littered the street in front of us, and our best chances were to not be seen. Hiding behind the buildings would definitely be our best chance of survival. We heard the distant howls of John screaming out several numbers at random.

A leaper jumped down from one of the buildings and went for the sergeant's leg. It bit down, broke its teeth and looked at his limb in confusion. It opened its mouth again to bite with its toothless smile, but was shot three times in the head by Ray. "Stupid fuck."

We reached the end of the street. The facility was down the road and to the right-exactly where the horde was fighting Gleesty. Sol limped as he fired his gun in front of us, spraying at nearby ticklers and gigglers. The gigglers laughed every single time they were hit. They all watched, twitched and cackled at us before being hit in the head with a bullet. Gleesty flew down the street, winding away, slicing the pavement open with his fore-blades. He crawled back to us with a large smile on his face.

"Mutt!" he screamed.

I yelled back with a large smile, "Glee!"

"Nice lady friend you got there!"

I laughed out loud. Lala giggled. The other two men held their fire and watched Gleesty clear out the zombies on our street. When he turned to wave back at us, the boar leaped for him, hooked him with his nose and launched him in the air. Lala and Sol gasped.

The boar opened his mouth, revealing the disgusting sludge oozing out of it, waiting for Glee to fall inside to be gobbled up. Gleesty fell right inside his mouth, half of him dangling out. The beast attempted to chew him up with his massive jaws. A blade pierced the boar, then another. Then, several ticklers and leapers climbed on the boar as Gleesty hacked away at the flesh sentinel. The boar was tilted horizontally, then vertically. At least 30 zombies were piled up on top of my friend at this point.

DDRRRUUUFFFFFFFF. The sounds of his pistons went off.

They were fired up into the air, Gleesty spun like a drill. Zombie limbs fired out in all directions.

We heard John yell, "I give! I give! You win!"

When Gleesty landed, he crossed his blades and bowed at us as blood rained from the sky for several seconds. It was pouring down at him, us and the stomping John from the end of the intersection. John dropped his gun and carefully hugged Gleesty.

We walked towards them arguing. "You shot at me!" Gleesty said.

"It was an accident!" John yelled back.

"You unloaded a full magazine clip at my chest you asshole!"

"I was just testing you!"

Gleesty shrugged, "well, at least you look dashing."

"Oh, why thank you!" John tucked his arms behind him and smirked. "See, I like you more and more every day."

Smiles and laughs were shared as Gleesty picked me up for a hug. It looked like John was calming down. I scanned the rooftops. The Owls were gone.

"Buddy, move!" Gleesty grabbed John and leaped out of the way. A car flew at them, barely missing my two friends. It crashed down and slammed into a building. We all forgot about the minotaur. It was at the other end of the street. There it stood, rubbing his hoof on the pavement, lowering its head ready to intercept Gleesty.

"Comrades," Gleesty said. "I saved the best for last. Unless you want to take this one, John?" John shook his head.

The beast opened its mouth and spoke. "YOU. ARE NOT. HIM. BRING. ME HIM." He pointed to me. Then at John.

Gleesty looked at me, then back at the beast, as did everyone else. "Nah."

The minotaur laughed.

"Mutt, I think he wants your horse shoes," John joked.

"THEN YOU DIE." The beast roared. "You all die!"

It charged for Gleesty, who leaped up and received the beast, jabbing his right blade into the minotaur's shoulder. It was unaffected by this. The zombie grabbed Gleesty with its left hand and slammed him to the pavement. Gleesty yelled in pain. He tried to pry his fist off, but the second he removed it, the minotaur rammed his giant head into Gleesty, smothering his entire body.

"No! " John cried. "Get up! Get up!"

He shot up from the ground, one of the blades successfully slicing out one of the beast's eye. The hairy, rotting creature slapped Gleesty to the side of the building.

"Fine! Fuck you!" My friend yelled. Gleesty jumped up, sliced the telephone cable and grabbed the cut end. He landed next to the beast, who was tending to its eye. The cyborg held the large wire with his gigantic fist, sparks firing out and kissing his right cheek.

Gleesty whipped around the beast, did another leap and, while holding the electric vine, pierced it through the zombie's jugular. He brought the giant bull down with him, inserting the wire deeper inside the creature, feeding it up its throat and of the mouth. I could easily see that Gleesty was also taking the electrical current, but the minotaur had it so much worse. Gleesty ripped the monster's arm out, stood on its head and stomped it to the ground. He stomped and stomped, every single time he crashed his foot on its skull, sparks fired out of the minotaur's mouth as its giant teeth chipped and sizzled away. The bottom jaw burst into flames. It kept screaming and writhing from the neural and jaw damage. Then it let out a moo.

Gleesty howled with laughter and knocked over a fire hydrant with an arm. It splashed all over the convulsing minotaur. Gleesty shot up into the air, darted downwards and spiked himself into the minotaur. The street caved into the sewer line. They both toppled downwards into it as an explosion took place.

Sol ran over to check the scene. We all followed in. When we looked down, we saw the minotaur in several pieces. Gleesty looked up at us, covered in feces, blood and whatever else that was down there. "I really wish I could do this every single morning," he joked. "Grade Z beef."

"How many points?" John cried.

"You're the math whiz. You tell me." He slowly climbed out of the hole and greeted us with a low belly laugh and noogies.

"G," I said. "How do I fucking thank you?"

"Naw, my friend. It is I who should be thanking you. And I am sorry for turning Bill in."

"You should not apologize to us for the rest of your days," John said.

Lala giggled a little more. Gleesty looked into her eyes and to his surprise, wondered who the pink haired, blue-toothed female was in front of him.

"Mutt Barrows, is this?"

Lala nodded. Gleesty removed the odd liquid helmet, grabbed her little hand with his robotic gauntlet, bent over and kissed it. "What is your name?"

"Lala. I'm a friend of Mary's." She giggled and winked.

Gleesty lit up with joy. John removed the decapitated head off his face and showed us his twisted smile. Together we walked to the skyscraper down the road.

Eighteenth Chapter

Everyone felt safe around Gleesty. The juggernaut managed to eliminate several hundred enemies without any guns. But his appearance left me to feel sad for him. It was far too unnatural for a human to live like that. He seemed to like it, though, so more power to him.

The giant iron gates before us were breathing. Within the iron bars, the cloning facility stood. It was designed to look like a pyramid. Gleesty spoke about it a few times; they felt that cloning was another way of rebirth. This interpretation, probably for marketing purposes, lead to the Egyptian design of the place.

We kept staring at the gates, wondering how on earth they could be breathing. The hundreds of dead bodies in the streets didn't even give us a clue. We were so used to it by now. Then we saw it: the machine-gun turret system that was cleverly built between each heavy black bar. Every tiny barrel was smoking-the light rain that drizzled down on the burning metal made the gate sound like it was gasping at us.

A man emerged out of the pyramid and marched toward us. Eventually, the gates parted, and we were welcomed by the saluting soldier. He had a red square on his heavy black suit.

Sergeant Ray, Specialists Lala and Sol saluted back. Gleesty lifted his two right blades in the air and smiled.

"Officer Trent, Sergeant Ray reporting, sir!"

"As you were, Ray," The officer said. He sluggishly walked back to the pyramid, etching at us to follow him. He spoke as the rain slightly started to pick up. "We saw it all. It is unfortunate we lost those soldiers. We are running low at the barricades. Seventy percent of the nation is now infected."

I figured that Officer Trent was drunk at this point. His wobbling up the stairs and disregard for proper military gestures were enough evidence.

Sol gasped. "How far have they spread, sir?!"

"Canada's got them. Wyoming's got them. Arizona's got them. They aren't zombies anymore. They are demons. Nothing short of demons. My family is gone. My friends are gone. My soldiers are gone. There are 50 people inside of this building. Used to be 500." We all stepped through the doors, steam blowing in our faces. "Everyone else is gone. Millions of them. We've received information that the United Nations will begin using nuclear warfare in the infected areas. I don't blame them. United States and Canada are now isolated from the world. The Catholic Church has begun performing massive exorcisms. Islams, Jews and Christians are doing the same. Everyone is working together to stop the mess. For once, there is peace amongst humans in the world, and it won't last long when we humans are wiped out.

"Just about all the other humans are gone. Aside from me and a few others, the rest are clones. They're supposed to be the expendable wall."

We reached a laboratory. All scientists and soldiers remained in a saluting position. Officer Trent grabbed a bottle of whiskey from a soldier's hand and downed it. "I am the first in command now."

Sol and Ray looked surprised. Ray opened his mouth to speak, "but, my-"

"I'll say it again. They fled. I'm in charge. Sol, Ray, I'm sorry but you were summoned here to replace your parental figures."

We all looked at each other in confusion. Gleesty spoke. "Trent. Where is John's uncle?"

"Working on the project, Major. Listen, is the supply van still intact?"

Gleesty nodded.

"Wonderful. There's hope. Glee, same mission. We need the supply box here.

"I'm on my-"

"Not yet. There are matters to discuss. We must enlighten your friends."

John looked at Trent like a hungry kitten. He was begging for his uncle. I was content. Lala was here, but I was dying to tell her everything. Gleesty just wanted to kill.

"Gleesty, Ray, Sol, Lala- come with me. We must set up a network on Gleesty, you will all act as his guide while he is out there." They all agreed, their stiff, rough bodies saluted Trent. "Gleesty, are you fine with us setting up cameras on you? We will be securing access points with copters and transmitters so we don't lose your signal. I want to report all of our findings out there, and make sure you are alright."

Gleesty nodded, retracting his lower blades and raising a fist in the air.

"You two," Trent pointed at us. "Someone is expecting you. Down that hallway, please." He panned his finger to the right, down a long, red hall.

John grabbed my hand and off we went. There was nothing short of silence amongst the both of us. The drugs were probably still in his system. I was just plain nervous. I imagined Bill Strub, still in critical condition, in his real death bed, whispering and holding John before he passed on.

Several soldiers nodded to us as we speed-walked down the gauntlet. The red hall turned green. At the end of the green was a wooden door. No security. Nothing. Just a plain, wooden door with a simple door knob. John grabbed a hold of it, twisted, and pulled. And there he was.

The room had large black containers, tubes, bubbling vats, 20 guards, a gigantic cloning machine, several desks, and a very strange man sitting with his back towards us. Bill was shirtless. Near his shoulder was a bloody gauze. John slowly moved to him as Bill was writing something.

I examined his pale skin. Bill was surprisingly well built for his age. I mean *very* well built. His muscles looked cut and sculpted perfectly. On his skin were several tattoos. Random numbers, rectangles, spirals, symbols and letters all scrawled on him. All in thick black ink. It looked like giant black bugs were crawling all over him.

I walked up to the left side of him, John to the right. We watched him drawing. Bill sat there completely still, drawing a perfect circle. Inside the circle, he drew another one that was touching the brim of the former circle. He did this again, and again, and again. All of them were absolutely perfect. He continued until it was nothing but a giant black dot on the piece of paper.

Bill exhaled. "When...I-was-a boy. I was advanced in my thinking pattern. That's why my brother *loved* me. When Iwasaboy. I would do this all day in class. I would draw this little black dot and stare it it. I would use it as a method of escaping reality. Just stare, climb inside the black dot and into oblivion. Inside the dark spot, I meditated. I escaped my body and reaped the telekinetic tides. In this black spot, I saw the prophecy. I was the light inside the black ooze. I knew this day would come. That's where it all started for me. Then John's father died. A year later, I went mad. I joined a league of mathematicians, where they all thought of me as the clown. I couldn't figure any of the problems that they did! Their methods felt tedious! So I rewrote every single equation in a new way. I solved what they solved, but in other various methods. They were very impressed with this and immediately made me president. Then, something happened.

"They brought up Hilbert's Problems. Twenty-three problems, well, 24. I fell in love with infinity, axioms, Riemann, entropy, thermodynamics, constructs, metrics, sex, math, sex, infinity, death. Oh, God, it excited me. I was dead set on figuring everything out, even if it was too vague, I would try to develop it. I solved a great amount of them." Bill started shaking furiously. "I *wasted* two fucking decades on them! I lost the love of my life for metrics and physics! For the greater good, I thought. What greater good? There was nothing wrong with the world! Then, when I stumbled upon several secrets on transcendental numbers, oh, sigma, I was wet with glee." Bill started heaving violently. I took a step back and watched John aid him. "The fog, the radiation, that star, I was connected with all of it somehow. When I saved everyone's life, the Goresmiths exiled me. But I cannot blame them, I abused their policies, and many lives were lost in my research. I only wish they brought me back sooner. I am sorry, to the both of you." Bill's hand twitched, causing him to spill his whiskey. "Heh, Mother Earth is the only female I know that gets uglier when I drink. Ah, this cursed poison doesn't kill fast enough. I remember when I wanted immortality. Now we are close to achieving that. When nostalgia becomes taboo, immortality will flourish. How's that for a contradiction?" He laughed.

John looked at him and smiled. "We know about everything. Thank you."

Tears rolled down Bill's face. "My lock-box?"

"What lock-box?" John smiled.

Bill Strub laughed and laughed. His bipolar personality was something I strangely missed. Life was not the same without him.

"My nephew, you are one step closer to being a better man than I." Bill said.

"I want to help everyone, like you," John said.

Bill grunted. "No, no that's the wrong way, John. That's how this mess started in the first place. The need to help everyone has turned everyone lazy. It's why this orange cataract surrounds earth. That's what the Owls are doing right now. Trying to help everyone."

"But they want to get rid of everyone!"

"For the greater good."

"You can't be telling me that you agree with them?!"

"No," Bill shrugged and stood up from his seat. "But I understand them. What they do not understand that it isn't our time yet. Earth is still a baby, and its steamy shit-stained diaper is wet. They want to change the diaper. I want to clean it. I know I am going back and forth, boys, but you must listen. This world will always have problems. We've made big problems into bigger problems. It's like a scale. And that's what I hate about it. John, your friend Mutt here always had it." Bill looked at me. It felt like telepathy. The black circle on his paper, the prophecy, I recalled the dream that I had several nights ago.

"So bright," I muttered.

Bill smiled. "John, embrace the cycle, no matter how twisted it can become. Well, I should really stop preaching my politics, I'm sure the soldiers are getting angry with my opinions." He looked at the group of clones that surrounded them. "My John, I will be fixing what I started. Or, rather, what evil has started."

"But Bill, what else could you have possibly done 20 years ago?" John asked.

"It is not me. It is us. We could have been better people. We all saw where it was all going. Now the evil is here."

"Lucifer?" I asked.

"Well, yes, that asshole might be to blame, but I do not blame him. No, not me. Blame greed. Everyone as a single person must take the blame."

"What are you going to do?" John asked.

Bill walked up to the giant cloning machine. It reminded me of a cauldron. He pressed a button and the cauldron's doors began to slowly open. Carbon dioxide was released; a mist that blocked our view of what was inside the chest. "I was going to create a special insolent to release in the mist, one that breaks down the neural chemicals and kills the sickness. But no, I'm tired of thinking inside of the box. It's time to bring the world back to what it was decades ago.

"I've been working on it for a long, long time. He is almost done. Soon, the madness will end." Bill raised his arms in the air with delight.

"I'm sorry," I said. "But what is the plan, Bill? The insolent in the air sounds brilliant."

His chuckling startled me. "Years ago, I was exiled for stealing certain objects. That's why the Goresmiths decided to pin the apocalypse on me 20 years ago. I had a solution for the miasma. There was a method to my madness, but they didn't believe me. They took Negativium and mass produced it, hoping that one day everything would be okay. They wanted the long way out."

"Oh my God," John's glare was horrifying. I looked at the cloning container and saw a man in the green fluid. I scratched my head.

"What kind of things did you steal?" I asked.

"The Shroud of Turin."

"What? What's that?"

"Oh, it's a cloth. It is thought to have the blood of a special man on it."

I started to get the plan now. I've never heard of this artifact before, or why Bill would ever steal it. I turned to John, who had a large smile on his face. "Are you cloning Lucifer to box him?"

John burst out laughing. I do know that Bill Strub is a professional boxer. He always had a thing for physical competition. But I knew my idea was completely wrong.

"Mutt," John said. "A little while ago the cloth, while its origins and time are still unknown, is thought to have the blood of Jesus on it."

Bill watched me, waiting for his reaction while coiling his gray mustache. His black eyes just waited for me. Then it hit me: Bill has decided to clone a prophet, a divine healer, a martyr. Insanity. The central figure of several religions was inside of a vat in front of me.

"Jesus. Fucking. Christ." I was shocked. "You have got to be fucking kidding me."

"I'm afraid not," Officer Trent said. Sol, Lala and Ray walked inside of the room. "This is the project."

"This?!" I yelled. "You are relying on something that could be a myth?! That's absolutely appalling! "Isn't his second coming supposed to raise the dead, bring forth judgment and-"

"Mutant," Bill said. "Look around you.

"Twenty years ago a fierce curtain of radiation nearly killed us all. The sky roared. I predicted it all. I predicted this. I could have stopped this infestation, but everyone was against me. The man in that big jar will determine what to do, because I refuse to take any steps further without him."

"Determine what to do? Do you even have an initial plan when he comes out of that chamber?"

"We're going to kill him."

I took a step back. Lala and John looked a little confused with this statement as well. Sol, Bill, Trent and

Ray all looked at me. Bill Strub continued, "Heaven's gates are closed. Everyone is damned. Demons walk the earth. Humans-they have slowly morphed into monsters because of an illness. The illness itself is a damn sin. It started as a sexually transmitted disease. Sin after sin, finally, one has sparked the end."

"So you're going to kill him." Lala said.

"I'm sure he will explain it much better than I when he awakens. For the greater good, his divine light must be shown for our path. Let there be light! And there was light, and it was good and bright. So bright."

"And where is God while all this is happening then, huh?" John said.

Bill walked up to John and clocked him on the head with his fist. "Like a said, my nephew, everything that is happening is our fault. The sin. God can't do anything because we did this to ourselves. He cannot just *come* down here and fix our problems. There is a reason he gave us free will."

"Okay, point taken," I said. "So God can't do anything because sinners must help themselves. Okay, I will pretend that that is how the rules are. Now, what makes you think this Jesus clone is going to fix everything when he is killed? Are you going to shoot him in the head the second he takes his first breath of air? This almost sounds like a really twisted Groundhog's Day."

Lala and John nodded.

"We shall crucify him," Bill said. "But we are going by the rules. If he understands that he is Jesus, we shall ask him if what we are doing will work."

John stopped Bill again. My friend lifted his head up as if he was ready to take another hit. "Clones do not have memories when they are hatched. They are programmed to understand their lives with the use of brainwave and memory machines recorded from the parent and then transferred over. When he is ready, won't he just be a confused, mindless drone?"

"No," Bill said. "Excellent question though. If he really is divine, then he will have the full understanding of what he is, and the same knowledge brought forth by God. If God makes this so, then we have a 'yes it will work' on our hands. If nothing happens, then we are screwed."

"So if this clone comes out and says 'hey, I'm Jesus of Nazareth, let's drive nails inside of me,' then we win?" Lala asked.

"Indeed."

"Bill," I said.

"Yes?"

"How did all of this come to be? It's like a nightmare."

"Please remember that dream, Mutt. While we are not controlled by fate, we are sometimes guided by companions. They cannot do everything for us. They can at least hold our hand and tell us that what we are doing has hope."

"I'm sorry, I need more proof."

"Look outside," Gleesty said, as he emerged out of the wooden door. "Officers, I am ready to roll out."

"No," I said. "Gleesty, this all seems far too unreal for me. It's like a bad acid trip."

"No shit, it isn't sunshine and rainbows out there, it is sickness and purgatory. The sea of metal is drowning us fishes."

"Ugh," I pressed the palm of my hand to my forehead. "How long until he is ready?"

"Six months if Gleesty fails."

"What do you mean *if Gleesty fails*?"

"The truck that you were all in had a special machine inside," Trent said. "It rapidly speeds up the clone's growth process. Inside, the machine produces a special chemical, it was too big for helicopters to transport."

"He was made with serum?"

"No, he is full blooded. It took several weeks of chromosome replicating and DNA reconstruction to perfect a single blood cell of his. It was very difficult with him, not to mention that he's been dead for over 2,000 years, but his blood is irradiated. He needs a specific steroid and abnormal proteins."

"His blood is irradiated," I shook my head.

"We're not sure if it's because of the cloth's exposure to fire over the years. We couldn't even use carbon dating to tell what time this damn thing is from," Trent said. "But as of now, this is all we have for you. "

"Those last few words are the scariest thing I have ever heard," Gleesty said with a chuckle.

"Everyone meet at the center of the facility when you are all ready. We will send out Gleesty shortly to recover the crate." Trent, Sol and Ray left. Lala walked close to me and smiled.

I couldn't help but feel sorry for her. She was caught in the middle of this and none of it was her fault. "I'm sorry about Mary," I said.

She looked down at the ground. "So, she's dead?"

"I'm not sure. She's definitely one of them though."

Lala shrugged and went back to her smiling. "We were parting ways anyway. I mean, it's still a shame that she's out there like that. But I really can't do anything about it. I'm probably a monster for thinking like this." She licked her teeth and let out a giggle.

I could feel Mary inside of her, but she still had something very different as well. I was shocked at her reaction. "Wait, what do you mean you were parting ways?"

"We both wanted different things." She looked at John and Gleesty, who promptly left us alone. Bill was far too busy to pay attention to us. "She didn't tell you why I'm here?"

"What?" I looked at her calm, warm eyes. She didn't have a care in the world. She looked content with her life, very tranquil. However, when she asked me that question, her expression mildly changed. She looked curious, interested in what I had to say. Interested in me. It felt right. "No, she said you just had to get some work done. I figured it was an early serum replenishment."

"No, no it's not like that anymore. I wasn't happy."

"With what?"

"Being fake."

"I really don't follow."

"Of course you don't, silly." She laughed. "I'm being ultra vague. My dear, I asked for a full blood transplant."

This shocked me. I didn't even think it was possible to convert to real DNA after the first initial copying process. Not only that, *why* convert to blood anyway?

"Why would you do that? And well, how?"

"They had to replace several organs so my body does not reject the blood. But hey, it worked."

"Okay, now why?"

"Because I want children," her face lit up.

There was a silence. Suddenly, she became completely serious. I liked it a lot. "And Mary didn't want this?"

"No, she didn't."

"Did she pay for this operation? I'm not sure why she would ever-"

"She owes me her life. I told her that I wanted to live my own life, without her. I mean, she's a great person, but we never got along very well. She just always wanted sex. Then one day, she overdosed on heroin."

Gwump. I swallowed. "And you got her off of it?"

"I kept her clean, yeah. The plan was to depart when she dropped me off here. I guess that's why she went to you."

Incredible. Mary broke up with her own flesh and tried to make amends with me. Everything felt so awkward. Awkward and veritable. In most cases, I find clones "fake." Plastic. They reminded me of Frankenstein's monster. The Tin Man. But this creature fooled me with her misleading exterior. Her passion for wanting to become a true human shined in itself. Her passion alone stood out from most humans who took their lives for granted. She is more human than I am.

It got me thinking. I consider myself a "true" human because I emerged from a womb? That's wrong, isn't it wrong? Is a mutant higher on the pyramid than the artificial living?

"I still would like to find her," she said. "She's still my friend."

"No," I said. "If we find her, the only way she can be your friend again is if there is some kind of cure. And from the looks of it, we are all counting on a psychopathic mathematician dadaist who tried to cancel out the universe at one point and is now attempting to clone a Jesus Christ of Newark."

Nineteenth Chapter

John and I are sitting behind a giant flat-screen monitor with several soldiers; this includes the rest of the infantry that sat with us in the large vehicle. It was a massive computer lab. We were still on the bottom floor of the building, only a few hallways from Bill Strub's chambers. Two scientists were setting up a camera on Gleesty's headgear when Bill rushed down the hallway screaming, "Black body radiation really fucked us this time, folks!" and passed out in front of the room from exhaustion. Two guards dragged him to his room to get some rest.

"The poor guy's been up for three days waiting for you to bring the chemicals and his family," Trent said. "Poor old man. Rushing to save this world that holds no merit to him."

Bill woke up a second later and screamed, "An evil, ultraviolet catastrophe! The bright epiphany is near!" It echoed to our room, which we all promptly ignored.

"So Gleesty must retrieve that big tanker thing that we were all in?"

"No," Ray said. "I mean, he probably could, but he only needs a specific box."

"Glee will also be showing off his skills while he is out there. So please watch closely." Gleesty extended his arms, showing off his four gigantic blades. "I'm pretty excited for round 2. Not gonna lie."

His body just wowed me. He flicked the lower blades that were attached to his cyborg arms back and forth like a dragonfly fluttering its wings. The swift clattering of a switchblade rang inside my head. He tucked the two gigantic upper swords behind his back. Something so divine surrounded his entity. The scariest thing about him was how quiet his body was. Quieter than my pink, wet human body. His didn't make any noise when he moved and turned.

"I think Mutt has a hard-on for me," Gleesty said.

"I'm pitching a tent myself," John said.

"Alright," Trent interrupted. "We have managed to set up access points to view the street cameras." He found a camera near the tilted truck and clicked on it. He sighed deeply when he saw all the supplies tipped over or shattered inside. Trent pointed to several objects inside that made him cringe. Gleesty muttered, "gonna hafta lick the bottom of our coffee mugs."

It was the late afternoon and we were all exhausted. Gleesty was the only one that was not affected by fatigue in the room. We shielded our eyes from his shining armor. No coffee, no real sugar, nothing to supply our bodies with some type of energy. The food reserves in this place were also running low, the supply truck that brought us here was meant to transport a biosphere, which is a full self-functioning farm that supported itself with several layers of important organisms. The bottom level of it contained organic wastes, while the middle held a spot for fish and plants, and the top layer had a mechanism for recycling soil with insects. Each level had a built-in light that helped the cells grow. What would be handy for us now was completely shattered in the streets, mixed with the dirt and the blood of the fallen soldiers.

"Glee," Ray said. "We need just enough to live for a handful of days. Trent has put me in charge of this entire mission while he gets some rest." Trent was already out of the room, yawning, waving good-bye to all of us. "If we do not get any of that growth serum back in our hands, we are probably going to starve to death before anything. The two-dozen soldiers and the rest of your friends are counting on you."

"Am I good to go?" Gleesty blurted.

Ray smiled. "Yep, enjoy your walk around the block."

Several scientists wheeled in the Jesus clone contained in the glass tube. They were transporting him to the elevator in the room in order to secure him to one of the revival chambers at the top of the odd building.

Gleesty looked at me, John and Lala. "Man, it sucks we haven't had time to talk about anything. But I'm sure mommy told you all about me."

"I'm really sorry about yelling at your family," I said. "I'm also sorry that neither of your friends have a car, a cell phone, health insurance or enough bullets in their gun."

Gleesty laughed. "We had quite an adventure, buddy. I just, you know, gotta make my family happy somehow. Okay, enough of this sappy shit, it's time."

Gleesty headed towards the secure exit. The camera turned on and we saw the the turrets and gates in the front court. He simply leaped over them and landed on the street. He stuck his thumb up in front of his face to assure that he was ready.

"Glee, you can always talk to us, it is built into the probe that we set up."

"Ah, cool, cool," he said as he performed a few cart-wheels.

"So what's the first thing we do when Jesus is here?" John asked. "Should we offer him gifts? Does he like mutated humans? Perhaps Mutt should leave."

"Bill said to just welcome him like a normal human being and wait for him to make the first move." Ray said. "Trent agreed, if he really is Jesus, he would already know about the situation."

Gleesty interrupted us with his singing:

Hum a mighty hum, hmmm-hmm-hm-hmm-hmmm.

Smile at the sun,

Rumm-pum-pum-hmm-hmm.

When you're on the run,

And you think you're done,

Just hum a mighty hum.

"I dare you to try and sing as low as him," John said with a curved brow.

Sol and Lala laughed. Gleesty was definitely a bass. His low vocals sent a soothing rumble down our spine. Everyone, including the guards from other rooms, rushed in front of the monitor to watch Gleesty in action. The first zombie was a giggler. It laughed and shook as Gleesty pierced 2 blades into its shoulders. He jumped up, taking the zombie into the air with him, twisting it around and stuffed the zombie between his legs. After several seconds of being in the air, he darted down and slammed the victim's skull into the pavement. It was completely unnecessarily for one little creature. I almost felt sorry for it.

He leaped about, traveling to other buildings.

"Gleesty, search for some Owls or civilians." Ray yelled at the monitor.

"I have a pulse sensor built into my system, man," Gleesty yelled. "And I only get the faint beats of the undead, baby."

Ray sighed and nodded. "Okay, alright. Just head for the tr-"

"Holy. Shit."

"What?"

"Big red dot, chief."

"A mutant?"

"Oh, fuck yeah."

"How far?"

"Seven blocks away. It's the only thing alive around here. A few news choppers are also circulating the area."

"Everyone's been saying that all of those things have been rushing back to New Jersey for something."

We all watched Gleesty as he swooped down through a car, shredding it and flinging the shrapnel at nearby enemies. Packs of zombies, now more than ever. The leapers clung to buildings and wriggled their heads left and right, taunting the cyborg viking. When one leaped at my friend, it was invited with a blade cutting it in half vertically. The rest followed in, some darting straight towards him. When they got to about a foot away from Gleesty, they were opened up in several pieces that fell to his sides.

He whistled. "Come!" He dug one of his blades into the ground. Gleesty twirled his body and whipped and sliced away at the zombies trying to flank him. The camera spun so fast that several soldiers affected by motion sickness vomited on the floor. Everyone cursed at Gleesty.

Once the enemies realized that there was no way to defeat our one man army, they ran away, darting down the street to a new area.

"They're heading for the red dot," Gleesty yelled. He leaped up onto a building, then to a few more. He reached his destination in less than 20 seconds. When he looked down from the building, he grunted. "How the *fuck* am I supposed to kill..."

Everyone's eyes were glued to the monitor. Several people placed their hands over their mouths and just shook their heads. It was the legion that we saw only a few hours ago. Only it was now the size of 8 school buses. Birds were swarming the area, feasting on the insects that were being spit out by the gigantic blob of flesh.

John pointed at a soldier. "Tell Bill that Abaddon has arrived." The soldier nodded and ran off down the hall and disappeared.

"So that's evil's weapon, huh?" Gleesty said. "Should I even-"

"No Gleesty," Ray said. Several other zombies leaped on top of the heaping mass of flesh to be absorbed. Its giant tentacle-like arms grabbed nearby buildings and trees and cars to move around. It was slow, but could move efficiently enough to get around to another street in several minutes.

"That's the ugliest fucking thing I ever saw!" Gleesty yelled. "Fuck you, ugly thing!"

Dozens of the legion's tiny eyes were looking at him. An arm was raised into the air, and hurled downward at the building Gleesty was standing on. It slowly started to crumble under his feet. My friend leaped down on the street to get a better look.

"Asshole," Ray's face was bright red with anger. He had to remove his army fatigues because he was sweating so much. "Just get out of there. I don't need you dead right now."

Then, an arm grabbed Gleesty and quickly whipped his body into the beast's large gap that acted like a mouth.

"Ragh!" was all he said before another arm twisted around his body and slowly lowered him into the large, wet, bloody crevice.

"Fight back! Get out of there!" Ray yelled. Everyone watched in shock and awe. "Just fucking do something!"

"Fine!" Gleesty yelled.

Hum a mighty hum...

My friend pulled out a hand grenade from a compartment built into his leg. He threw it inside the mouth and watched the beast coo and roar when the grenade blew up. The legion let Gleesty go, and as it did, my friend promptly picked up several cars, trees and pieces of buildings and started spiking them on top of the legion.

Hmmm-hm-hmm-hmm-hmmmm!

He pulled out several other grenades, some looked different than others. From the point of view, we saw our friend salute the beast with a blade as he chucked more bombs at the thing. Bursts of lightning, flashes and fire consumed the thing, the cars on top of it blew up and the fog and dust made it nearly impossible to see. Gleesty quickly left the scene.

"Nevermind, it's still on my sensor. No way I could take that. We need an air strike. Where the fuck is everyone?"

"Pay attention," Ray said. "Every single military unit has been deployed to Canada's borders."

"Why?!"

"If we do not oblige to the United Nation's requests, we shall be terminated."

"That's not fair at all! We can't leave, we can't defend ourselves, so what the fuck?!"

Heavy winds picked up on Gleesty's camera. Shrapnel whipped and rust forming a sandstorm, waves of orange and brown blocked out camera view.

"Why couldn't we just send for another supply truck?" I asked.

"Would've taken days," said Trent. "And if this epidemic is not contained within a month, they will bomb us anyway."

"There is just no way. But Bill has a plan!"

"They will do it."

Static and white noise muddled the one-man army's microphone. The storm went on for another twenty seconds. When it cleared, we could hear trumpets. Several news choppers were surrounding the area. This was the hot spot, the area that the world was paying attention to.

"I found the crate," Gleesty's voice pulled through. We could see him pick up a box, about four feet in length and four feet in width, with his two mechanical arms. When the camera panned upwards, we witnessed the Owls playing their trumpets to the swarms of zombies leaping inside of the legion's mouth. Thousands charged at the giant flesh beast as it coiled and consumed a skyscraper within minutes. Zombies were just being absorbed by it instantly.

Terror filled everyone as Gleesty backed several feet away. Owls tumbled down into the heaping mass of flesh as it slowly grew to ridiculous proportions.

The beautiful owl that I ran into days ago looked at Gleesty and smiled from her building. "Mystery," She screamed, "Babylon the Great, The Mother of Harlots and Abominations of the Earth!" She dropped off the building and into the creature's mouth.

"No time to waste," Gleesty yelled. "Get the subject ready. If he isn't hatched in an hour, it is over. This is it."

Twentieth Chapter

They explained to us that there is a hidden chamber underneath the building that is linked to an abandoned underground sewage tunnel. An old cart will guide us down a railroad track far enough to escape the mayhem. I doubt it.

Lala grabbed my hand as the 8 of us; Trent, Sol, Ray, Lala, John, me and two soldiers headed to the second of the three floors. It was a big, open room filled with surveillance and a handful of scientists cursing at each other. The sweat on their foreheads shined from the red light given off by the emergency signals.

Bill emerged from behind a large machine with a large smile on his face. He pointed at John and asked him to come to his side. Everyone else broke free of the group and found a spot to keep busy at. Lala stayed in the middle of the room with me.

"What happens if he isn't Jesus?" I asked.

"Well, we die, right?" Lala asked.

"Probably, but what should we do if the plan fails? Do we just run?"

"Nah," she shrugged. Her freckles shined under her lightly wrinkled eyelids. The blue sapphire freckles overpowered the red lights. Omnipotence; if I could bow to her without looking insane, I would. "We'll run away together, just us. Hide in the underground sewage until that thing leaves, and we can flee on boat to a new area. We can have kids, we can start over on an unknown land and let the rest of the Earth rot."

I stared at her. When she blushed, her freckles turned purple.

"I'm sorry," she said, "Just a dream."

"I'll follow you anywhere you'd like."

We both smiled as I began to caress her hair.

Gleesty burst through a window a few seconds later, plowing over anything that stood in his way. He tore open the crate and grabbed the contents. Lala and I watched John and Bill talking in sign language for absolutely no reason at all.

"How the fuck do I set it up?!" Gleesty yelled.

Bill guided him straight to a machine where the clone was held. He inserted the red liquid into a tube and waited for something to happen. Everyone was leering at Bill. So many lives depended on this moment.

Trent walked over to Gleesty and grabbed him by his shoulder. "Glee, I have to tell you something."

"What is it, man?"

"Your dad was on the news. Everyone else is fine. Odradek had a stroke. He's been up for 4 days and has been taking excessive Modafinil."

Gleesty frowned. "He can't. Not now." He looked down. I went over to him, waiting for him to look up.

"Don't worry, Glee," Trent said. "He'll be okay as long as the zombies do not break through the walls."

We heard John's voice from across the room. "Bill, how long will this take?"

"He technically *is* ready. The drug that I gave him was to make sure he doesn't die of shock when he wakes up. He's been fed constant hormone and aging supplements to accelerate his aging. No clone has ever reached this age this fast. But I want it perfect."

"So, how long, assfucker?"

"Ten minutes."

Gleesty looked up at Bill. "Bill, you have 5."

"Blast. My friend, I assure you that your family will be fine."

"I know that," Gleesty said, sticking out his chest. "But we won't be."

He pointed to one of the screens monitoring above the rust. It was there, a gigantic, hovering ball of despair. Tens of thousands of zombies, buildings, cars, wires, pipes, all floating in a disgusting force of otherworldly hatred. The bodies clung onto the exterior of it like puppies nibbling on their mother's breasts. The legion sucked in the fog at an alarming rate, growing even more powerful. It was only 8 blocks away, two hundred feet in the air.

"Behold, the egg that will hatch our demise," Bill shouted. He turned around and slammed his fist down on a button encased with glass. "Rise!"

The fluid inside the clone's container began to drain. The tubes sticking out of him began to pump and suck. Carbon dioxide released from all corners of the project. Everyone watched and waited for the answer.

The upper and lower shafts of the container slid out and were lifted up by a separate machine. As the big glass cylinder rose up, it took the small rubber tubes with it. The man was now standing upright all by himself. His eyes were still closed. His arms were still by his side. Lifeless. Just a naked, lifeless man.

And then he exhaled. An aged breath of warm air filled the room, soothing us, burning the metal in our eyes. I shut mine as they began to tear. I wasn't crying because of the breathing, I was crying because for that second, I felt safe. I felt like I was in front of the only person worth thanking to be alive. The room was filled with an empowering glow. Our heart's spirits were shrieking, "We are men! Look at us!"

And then he opened up his eyes. That second was the most important second of my life, only to be shadowed by the moments coming thereafter. This was the moment we were all waiting for. There was no look of confusion on his face.

His eyes scanned the area. He breathed in. Everyone smiled and gasped. Commonly known, the first reaction of a clone being brought to this world is a facial expression of befuddlement, followed by an anxiety attack. Not here. He looked certain and sincere.

Everyone got on their knees, and thanked him, our Holiness. He took a step forward and opened his mouth to speak. All eyes looked at his mouth and waited for his first words. "Not this shit again," He muttered.

Bill laughed while others were so surprised that they almost fell over.

"No," Jesus said, "come on, seriously. I know exactly what's going on here. And damn it. You are all assholes."

"But," Trent said. "Please, I'm sorry, we are very confused."

"Confused?!" he yelled. "I am the all-knowing son of God! I know exactly what you want to do to me. Well, let me ask you this: What makes you think that I will succumb to your demands?"

"Okay, let's nail him!" Bill yelled.

Jesus looked at Bill. "Really, Judas? Fucking really? Bringing out the hammer already? You can kill me, but it won't do shit to help you."

"So, my plan won't work?"

"No."

"But, I don't understand."

"That's a first! Look at you. Listen, none of you are worthy of being saved by me. Do you now understand? I must consent to my martyrdom in order to save you all."

"Ah," Bill said. "I see. So we can't be saved unless you want us to be saved. And you don't want us to be saved."

"There you go."

Bill shrugged and grabbed a gun. "Well, plan failed. Time to kill you."

"No!" John dove for the gun and wrestled with Bill. He pulled it out of his white, wrinkly hands. "Jesus, excuse my uncle."

"Excuse yourself, maniac. John, don't think good maniac-bad maniac trick will work with me."

"Aw, shucks." John swung his right arm at the air.

"Well," Bill said, "we tried."

"Wait," Gleesty said. "Both of you knew that he was going to be a pessimistic, anti-human, stubborn-person?"

They both looked down. "Well," Bill said. "He didn't look very happy in my dream."

The rest of us scratched our heads. Jesus looked over to a monitor. "Oh! The legion has arrived!" He waved at the screen.

A dark, deep voice filled the sky. The building rumbled with a ghoulish presence.

What do you plan to do, Jesus of Nazareth? You are too late.

Jesus shrugged.

Sol ran up to Jesus and grabbed him. "Listen, I don't care who the fuck you are, but we have to get out of here, and I'm not leaving anyone behind!"

"Oh, fine," Jesus said.

Two elevators were being operated to bring us all down. The scientists and remaining soldiers ran to the opposite side of the room as the 9 of us waited for them to access the hidden door in the floor.

The entire building shook. It slowly started to cave in. As it crumbled, we could not see the remaining soldiers or scientists. Dust and metal twisted around us as it was sucked up by the beast. It pulled off the top of the pyramid. Lala was screaming on the floor, and when she looked up, she saw the big black beast with its prisoners. It was gigantic, almost twice the size of the Goresmith's headquarters.

"Fuck it!" Gleesty rammed his fist through the floor and blasted it open. He pulled out the door and flung it into the air. We all ran down the stairs. Jesus was still loafing around.

"Down here," Trent yelled. We all rushed down the tunnel. I felt the gravitational force of the legion, pulling me towards it, asking me to join the army. At the end of the tunnel, a large vault door was found. Gleesty turned the large wheel and opened it with no problem.

"Fuck," Ray said. "They should have just bombed us sooner!"

"Yep, genocide is always the answer," Jesus said sarcastically. "Ethnic cleansing kits in every household. You all never fail to impress me."

Lala looked at him and tried to smile. He shrugged at her. "Freak."

The seven of us climbed down the hole. Jesus and I were last. I stopped him before he jumped down.

"Oh," he said with a large smile on his face. "Sorry, after you. The donkey accompanying me on my last journey always had his head first."

The destructive burps from the legion were heard outside. I thought about every single person that died these past few days. I thought about Mary crying, all the people crying, I thought about poor Baxter. This asshole knew who they all were and was by no means sought to help out any of them.

"Come on, guys!" Sol said. They all looked at Jesus and me from the ledge below the vault.

"No," I said. "Hold on, why are we running? We have the key right here to stop it all. And he isn't looking to relieve us of our problem. He knows he's going to die, so what does he care?"

Jesus laughed. His beard curled in the faint light from the very few bulbs hanging down from the ceiling.

"Why can't God help us?" I asked. "Let's get the main question out of the way. If I'm dying, I at least want to understand what's going on."

"Oh my God, you can talk!" Jesus laughed.

"Answer the question, please."

"Alright, fine."

"Let me guess," John said. "God hates us?"

"Actually, no, I won't say that. I'll tell you the truth. My dad gave you all free will. That was the unique gift that he gave all of you. Are ya with me? It was something that fascinated him, to watch unpredictable beings that aren't under his control. He did set up his own rules and jurisdictions. First of all, yes, these demons all sprouted from sin. A tiny little sin in a tiny little virus. And it spread. It spread to an ultimate evil. This evil evolved in a very impressive amount of time. It evolved and strengthened from the sinners. And that thing will one day hatch out an old friend of my fathers. Follow? Okay, good.

"He would have helped you all. Over two decades ago, the devil came around with a wager for God. Lucifer was really angry at the sudden use of clones. He could see it in God's eyes that he also did not like where it was going. And do you know what my father said?"

"He hates us?" John said.

"No. God said: If they want to play God, let them play God. But can these tiny little super-beings prove to be as powerful as I with a test?

"And the Devil laughed. He asked God for two chances to stop the human race. The first plan was God's choice; the radiation wave, to see if his little friends on earth could defeat a typical Armageddon.

"But Lucifer's idea was a little different. Instead of a gigantic tidal wave of destruction, he went for something so small that our naked eyes could not see. They agreed for a 20 year gap, a chance for you all to heal from God's plan then face the Devil's plan. Of course, God and Lucifer agreed to warn a single human, that Judas fellow over there."

"That is terrible," I said.

"Mutt!" Jesus yelled. "It's now a god-eat-god world. You're all godlike now, great. Technology has proven to make you all immortal, all-powerful and all-knowing. And look at what you've done with it. War, famine, sex and death. Science and faith has failed you all. Try harder next time." His arms fell to his sides. The look of dissatisfaction was smeared across his face.

Appalled and shattered, I looked down at all of the people who accompanied me on a hopeless journey. There they all were, sitting in a hole, afraid and dirty. Beyond the hole I could see nothing; and the faces of my friends remained quiet and sad. All demoralized, except for John and Bill, both with their hands in a praying position. Gleesty set his blades down and looked at the ground, wondering if he should climb back up and get sucked up by the legion. Lala, Sol, Trent and Ray dropped their weapons and waited for doom.

John stopped praying and threw my old backpack at me. Inside contained three things: my gun, Bill's book, and a white rose. My gun was refastened to my holster, still with that final bullet. The book I kept under my left arm, and the rose I handed to Jesus.

The scent of the rose opened up my veins. I felt the warm hum of bees and a strange soothing flow of honey down my back. Outside, I was relaxed. Inside, I was enraged. I either use my final bullet on my prophet, or I use the knowledge that I accumulated over my adventure.

"Do I look like a god to you?" I asked Jesus. His eyes widened. "Look at me! I've been an outcast my entire life. My family was an outcast, my friends are outcasts, I've been looked down at from every street corner, rooftop and sewer! So a god-child looking down at me right now doesn't mean a thing to me. That look you have in your eyes right now is something that I've seen for almost two decades. Do you know what that tells me? It tells me that you are no different than anyone else that I've come across.

"But that never stopped me. I don't want to give up on this world! Tomorrow might be the greatest day of my life! And I will happily die the day after if that prediction came true.

"And I look at you, those fucking eyes again. You are just like every other human that existed last week, a dirty sinner waiting to tear apart the world because of your anger. You've tried to help this world once before, and you succeeded. And now, what is your excuse?" My voice echoed in the halls. My voice was so loud, the rumbling chaos from outside was eliminated and replaced by my screaming. "That it's too late? That we've failed? Failed what? My entire life I thought that you were made up, so you looked down at me because I didn't know the truth? In this day and age, how could I believe you existed without any evidence? You cheated yourself. I can't *believe* that I love humans more than Jesus Christ himself, and I'm a mutant that has been spit on more times than I have smiled. Go ahead, hang me on the cross. I will gladly die for these people."

By the time I shouted the last sentence, his arms were around me, holding me. He let go, a look of confusion was on my face until I saw his tears.

"And that was the third test we agreed on," he said. "Thank you for not letting me down, my son."

He leaped down with the rest of my companions and apologized. He noticed Sol's wound on his leg, touched it and it healed instantly.

"Incredible," Bill said. "I was afraid of going through with the other plan."

"What other plan?" Trent said.

"To summon the great Cthulhu to battle the legion. Then kill it when the opportunity would come around."

After I jumped down, Gleesty shut the vault. Everything was dark, until Gleesty turned on this light on his chest. The place was dirty, cracked and smelled horrible. We walked a few feet down, found a door, and entered it.

Inside was a room the size of my apartment. There were other doors that were either barred up or locked. Gleesty and the soldiers cut the bolts down or shot at them with their rifles. I found a light switch and flicked it up. Several lights turned on and we started to worry less. A breath of relief came from all of us when we found bottles of water and canned food in a closet. More importantly, we found a radio.

Sol turned it on and we all listened.

This message will repeat for the next hour. Let it be known that the virus has not only spread through Canada, but has breached Europe as well. The United States has failed to hold the virus within the country. Because of the sudden breach in Europe, firebombing will begin at the infected borders shortly. Several missiles have been aimed directly at the giant threat in our nation. A full-on attack on the giant monster will being shortly. All civilians must try to flee to a high area or to the shores. This is an emergency bulletin uploaded through all radio stations. This message will repeat for the next hour.

"Chaos like nothing else," Ray said. "So, now what?"

Trent pointed to a door that we did not open just yet. "That's the exit. Inside is a speed-cart built on old subway tracks. But guys, what's the point on moving? That big thing is going to swallow the earth."

"No," Jesus said. "Have faith in me. The night shall pass."

"But father, what could you do against all of this? Against that over-demon? I can't believe I just called you father," Trent said.

"My son, let my Transubstantiation take place. My body shall overcome the ailments. My blood shall wash away the evil. I will terminate the plague."

"I cannot imagine this all to be reversed."

"It can be," I said. The dream I had when I slept with Mary was ringing in my head. Jesus had a special energy surrounding him, unseen, but it could be felt. Something divine was inside him, screaming to emerge.

"The energy that our lord and savior has suppressed is unique," Bill said. "I've been monitoring his irradiated blood for a few months. He is immune to the rust. It breaks down in his system, unlike us. That should be a good enough hint to what will happen."

Jesus nodded. John looked around enthusiastically. His fingers tingled with determination.

Trent smiled, for the first time this entire mission, I saw his big, toothless, ugly smile. "That cart can only fit six people. There are nine of us. I will stay and operate the power, to make sure everything is intact. Who will join me?"

Sol and Ray saluted, ready for action.

"Very well, no time for small chat then! Let's give these heroes a chance to save our asses!"

"Yes, sir!" A roar from the two soldiers. Their echoes were so loud in the room that it sounded like 80 finely trained warriors giving their battle cry. Jesus touched both of their chests and thanked them.

We exited the room and we all arranged ourselves in the cart. Gleesty managed to set himself up in the front, along with John and Bill. Then it was Lala, Jesus and me in the back. The cart had a small manual steering wheel in front of it, but Trent said it won't be needed; he will set up coordinates to our destination.

"Well, where are we going?" I asked.

"There are several paths, but we are taking you to Hoboken."

"What for? What exactly are we doing though?"

"The rust in Hoboken has subsided," Gleesty said. "Hardly any zombies there."

"Then that is where I shall be released," Jesus said.

"Everything is ready to go. Let this be a goodbye." Ray pressed a button and we were fired out down the rail. Sol and Trent saluted and ran inside the underground safe room.

"Jesus," I said. "Now that you are here, can you answer me the big questions?"

"Depends on the questions," he said, laughing.

"What happens to clones when they die? Are they permitted to go up *there*?"

"Clones are people too. And yes, don't worry. Your loved ones will be with you. And to be honest with you, I am only a copy of the former Jesus."

"There will be two of you?"

"No, our souls will merge. It's a little complex, but do not fret."

"I don't want to ask why we are here, or anything too broad, I feel I am lucky enough to already have met you on earth," I laughed. "Doubt you'll answer most of them anyway."

"Well, Mutant, let me say that I am honored to have met you. There is a spot up there for you, somewhere."

I looked at John, who was glaring at me. "Sorry Jesus, but my Heaven is beneath my feet."

He laughed and John sighed with relief. Gleesty sang, "Val-Halla!"

Lala was looking right at Jesus, still speechless. She finally spoke to him, "Is Mary dead yet?"

Jesus shook his head. "No, she is out there."

"Can we bring her back?" She asked.

"Yes. I shall amend this Earth. You will all take place in my crucifixion."

"Why would you want such a cruel way to die?"

"I cannot imagine another way of death for me. History does indeed repeat itself, and I must follow in with my destiny."

Gleesty turned around to face the divine being behind him. Something was bothering him. "If you exist, then the Norse worlds do not exist. How will I meet my ancestors!?"

Jesus patted his head. "There are Vikings in Heaven too, silly."

Gleesty shut and smiled, nodding kindly to his new friend.

"Gleesty," John said. "Thank you for protecting us. You've carried such a burden this entire time, and I must tell you how much I appreciate it."

"My friends," he said. "You have all kept my life far from boring. I am honored."

The cart stopped. Not because there were any problems, but we reached our destination. The lights were flickering, and we could barely see the ladder from up above. After the ladder was another vault. Gleesty leaped up and ripped it out of the socket. After the horizontal vault door was a manhole. This "secret", supposedly secure sewer line lead to a street.

"Let's go!" Gleesty yelled as he pressed the manhole out. The second it popped out, we heard the screeching of nearby zombies that have not yet been absorbed by the legion. "Hold that thought." The cyborg leaped up onto the street. We heard his blades slicing around for several seconds, then silence. "Alright, let's go again!"

Lala, Jesus, Bill, John and I climbed up and saw the chaos outside. The air was lighter than usual. Most of the buildings were demolished, and the air smelled of sulfur. Small fires scattered the streets. I looked at Jesus and saw how torn up he was.

"I'm sorry," he said. "I should have been prepared to see something like this. I've seen the cruel famines and plagues for centuries, but it still sickens me."

He pointed to a grassy hill that was about a half-mile away. Suddenly, a small beam of light shined onto it. The clouds and fog cracked opened and shined enough light to surprise me. This was the first time I ever witnessed real sun light in the streets on New Jersey. I felt like I was on the tallest building. Sunlight. It was amazing.

"It shall happen there."

Behind us, an army of moans clawed at our backs. When we turned, we saw the legion flying very low to the ground. It must be almost a mile long now. Hundreds of birds and insects surrounded it, flying in circular motions.

"Better happen fast!" Gleesty said. Demons poured from underneath the legion. The little mouths on the gigantic sphere of pestilence shouted and hissed at us; bleeding, vomiting, crying, all mouths commanding their hordes of creatures, sicking them at us. They were only a few miles away, we had very little time.

Gleesty saw an abandoned trailer attached to a crashed truck. After ripping the trailer free, he motioned for us to get on. We leaped onto the wooden platform as he pulled it as fast as he could to our destination. "I can't believe you wanted to do it there!" He yelled. "Why there, Jesus?"

"It's lovely," Jesus said.

We must have been going 50 miles an hour now. We were there in a few moments. Not far from us was our major threat.

"You, Metal One, break two boards from the platform," Jesus ordered Gleesty, who promptly followed his directions. It was obvious why Jesus wanted these two wooden boards. I grabbed a lengthy metal wire and wrapped it around the two boards until it made a letter T. Gleesty pushed me back, tied it as tight as possible and laid the giant crucifix on the ground.

Lala weaved several green branches of poison ivy and adorned the crown with barbed wire and placed it on His head.

Jesus rested on the crucifix. He extended his arms out and closed his eyes. "Blessed are the pure in heart, for they shall see God."

Terror was all I felt. The innocent man was here ready to sacrifice himself to us.

"Do not worry, Mutt. I do not feel forsaken. I am your blessing, your weapon. In this, our finest hour, I do not regret my death. I will not die in vain!"

Gleesty rolled up several pieces of metal with his bare hands, forming nails. By the time he finished, we heard the burning desire of the demons.

"Unclean spirits!" They yelled. "Join the Wicked Generation!"

Gleesty turned to all of us. "I will handle them. I am counting on you to set this up." And he leaped down the hill, spinning into his chaotic dance. The legion was now closing in, we had very little time.

"Mutt, please!" Jesus yelled. Bill handed me the nails as I grabbed a rock and drove a metal spike into his left wrist. He howled in pain. My tears landed on his bloodied arm as I moved to the other side and drove another nail in with one single blow. More screaming. Before I could react, I stuck another nail on the top of his right foot. By this time my hands were trembling. Lala and John patted Jesus' head and cried. Bill grabbed one side of the cross and prepared to lift up after the final nail.

I blacked out for a second because of the terror. When I looked down, the final nail was in. When I turned to look at Gleesty, a loose zombie dove for me.

John pushed me away and grabbed the bloody demon. It sunk its teeth into John's shoulder. He yelped from the pain. Belligerent, John pushed the zombie away, knocking it to the ground. Something popped in John's brain. He leaped onto the zombie, and started gnawing away at the neck.

"How do you like that?!" He said, cackling in an outstanding rage. He ripped out chunks of flesh with his teeth. "Cretins!"

I turned to Lala and Bill, who were holding Jesus in the air. If they were to let go, he would tumble down.

"Jesus, now what?!" I screamed.

Lala and Bill managed to push the cross into the dirt deep enough for Jesus to stay up freely.

He was suffering tremendously from his wounds. He opened up his eyes. "Kill me." He mouthed.

Lala and Bill both looked at me with sad eyes. I nodded and continued to weep.

I removed the gun from my holster.

I turned to Gleesty who was slowly becoming overwhelmed by the horde. The legion's shadow consumed the entire area. The sun was blocked, the moon was gone. The only light we had was the pillar of energy from Jesus. The curtain of light was all we could see in the horrific night.

I looked at John, blood stained all over his face, breathing in the rust fragments through his nose.

"Weapon of Destiny," Jesus muttered.

I kissed the barrel and pointed it at the chest of Jesus. I pulled the trigger. The echo of the explosion silenced everything on Earth. The bullet escaped the gun and entered His chest. He struggled from the pain for a second, and looked at me with a smile.

"It is finished." His last words.

An explosion of violent blue light fired into the sky, knocking us all back. The sound of an almighty crackle rung in my ears. I couldn't breathe, see, or speak. I could only feel an electric burn across my body as it was sent back down the crumbling hill as the nova engulfed everything.

A voice echoed.

So bright.

Twenty-First Chapter

Hm.

Where the Hell is that clock tower?